CW01647324

The Betrayal of Jacqueline Flower

Praise for the Author

About *'One Single Ticket'* by Robert Wallace:

"A detective story told at a breathless pace, with a Richard Hannay type hero straight out of a John Buchan thriller, and it goes with a swing"

Professor Angus Buchanan, author of 'Brunel: The Life and Times of Isambard Kingdom Brunel

"The plot is so interesting, and the setting so well done; a delight to get a scenic picture of this special event in history."

Dr. Gabrielle Obrist, Museum of Modern Art, Zürich

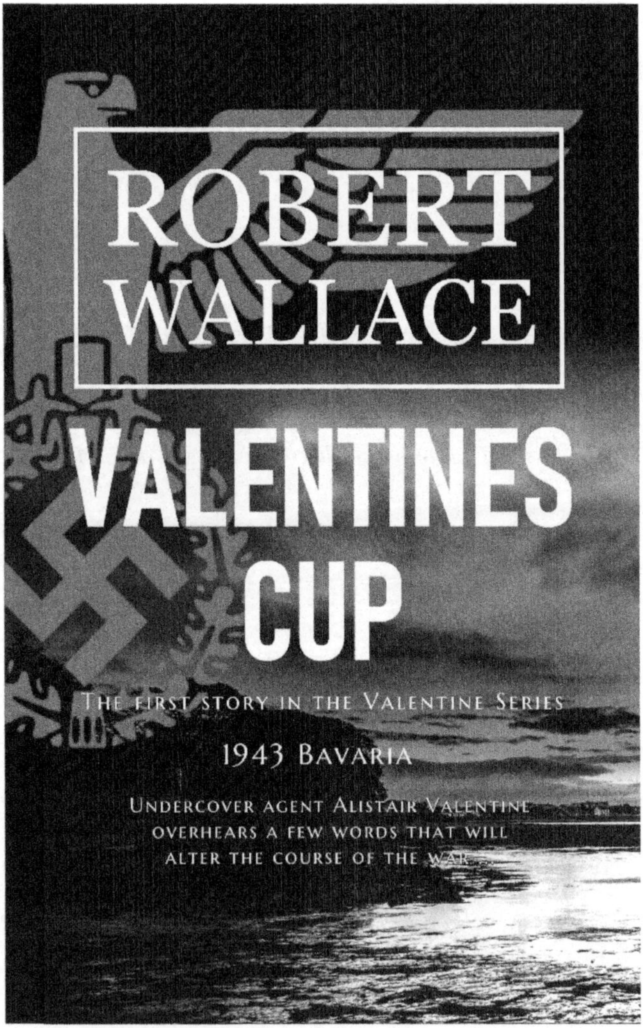
ROBERT
WALLACE
VALENTINES
CUP
The first story in the Valentine Series
1943 Bavaria
Undercover agent Alistair Valentine
overhears a few words that will
alter the course of the war ...

Also by Robert Wallace

The Valentine Series

Valentines Cup

Crimson Wing

Monkeypuzzle

Operation Gunfleet

Other novels

One Single Ticket

A Victorian detective thriller based on

real events and revolutionary ideas

from Isambard Kingdom Brunel

Fables and Folk

A collection of West Country supernatural short stories

The Betrayal of Jacqueline Flower

A psychological crime thriller with a twisting storyline

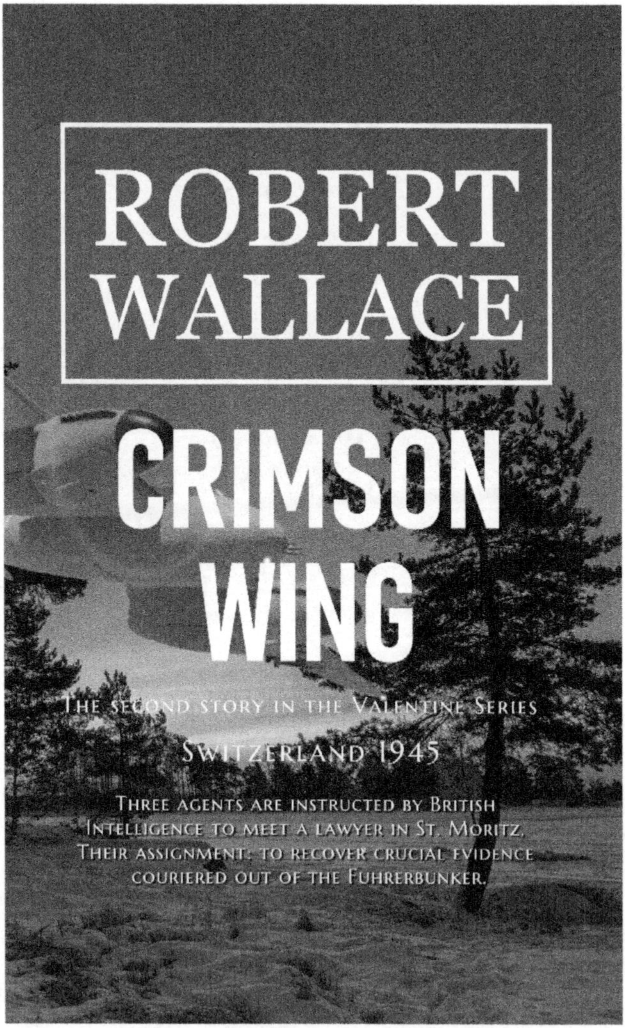
ROBERT
WALLACE
CRIMSON
WING
The second story in the Valentine Series
Switzerland 1945
Three agents are instructed by British Intelligence to meet a lawyer in St. Moritz. Their assignment: to recover crucial evidence couriered out of the Fuhrerbunker.

About the Author

Robert Wallace was born and raised in Bristol and spent many years working in the medical field which took him to Europe, the United States, Japan, Australia and Scandinavia. It sparked a lifelong interest in travel. His work involves turning historical events into works of semi-fiction, retaining the factual background, creating fictional characters to share their lives with real people.

ROBERT
WALLACE

The Betrayal of Jacqueline Flower

TradShack

Cover design by www. tradshack.com
Published by www. tradshack.com

ISBN: 978-1-7397822-6-9

In memory of my father Jerry Wallace
who was born 100 years ago today, 22nd October 1922;
and who sadly passed away 14th November 1976.
Always in my heart.

*'The leaves of memory seemed to make
a mournful rustling in the dark.'*

Henry Wadsworth Longfellow, 1807-1882
The fire of Drift-wood.
Devereux Farm, Near Marblehead, MA., USA.

Bathtub

Lafayette, Louisiana, USA.
Twenty years ago

THE CHILD IN THE BATHTUB cries a frenzy of uncontrollable sobs. Her mother Alicja scoops her from the water, wrapping a damp, stained towel around her shoulders, holding her in an inescapable hug. She rubs her back, gathers her wet hair to her breast. The child surrenders her tears to her mother, her fingers digging deep into her towelling bathrobe.

The bathroom windows of the old American house are shut tight, drenched with condensation, refusing entry to the outside world as witness to the events that occurred only moments ago. On the white-tiled floor tiles lies the twisted and motionless body of Bruno Kaminski, the girl's uncle. His skull is cracked open revealing a fresh route into that dark, salacious mind; or the escape route for the evil that haunted him.

Either way, if he's still alive it's a miracle.

"It's ok, Jax, baby ..."

But Jax is not ok. Her bare feet skid on the wet, blood-soaked floor tiles, her mother frantic with attempts to comfort her.

Alicja stifles her tears. "You're ok, Jax. We're back together now. It's alright. Hold me tight."

Jax clings to her mother, eyes wide with shock.

"Bruno won't touch you no more, baby. His time has come now, he's gone forever. But I had to see for myself, Jax. I'm sorry, I should have listened to you."

Jax stares at the lifeless, blood-soaked body and thinks: *yeah mama, you should have. The monster may be dead, but I'll never be free of him.*

Camden Town

London, England

NOW TWENTY-FIVE, JAX sits on the floor in her flat in London listening to Mozart's Piano Concerto No 21 on CD. She's browsing through a scrapbook containing newspaper articles. She turns the pages:

> *The Daily Advertiser, Louisiana, January 2003. 'Murder.' Copy about the cold-blooded murder of one Bruno Kaminski.*

> *New Orleans Advocate, June 2003. 'Woman convicted of second-degree murder. Alicja Donovitch pleads guilty and offers no defence.'*

> *The Daily Advertiser, Louisiana, July 2003. 'Killer of Kaminski commits suicide in Louisiana Correctional Institute for women.'*

Jax sighs, sips her coffee and flicks to the next page of the scrapbook: a memory she recalls only too well:

> *Charlotte Observer, September 2003. 'Myers Park High School holds their swimming gala.'*

A photo of the girls' team, all holding rosettes and their place ribbons for competing. Each contestant looks proud and holds their trophies with smiles. Jax sits on the end of the bench looking uneasy, she's holding a 'runner up' blue rosette. Her fear of water already evident.

*

Six years later her life was starting to improve. Her mother had left her a little money so she could afford acting lessons at a theatre school in Charlotte. Later, she appeared in plays throughout North Carolina.

One day after a matinee she was approached by two producers from New York. Blake and Amelia were scouting for a promising actress. Jax fitted the bill – right age, right face, plus she'd worked for WCCB and FOX TV stations. Amelia would find her a coach and pay for her to move to New York.

Gramercy Park is a quiet, well-to-do residential area with brownstones and tree-lined streets. Amelia found her a tiny apartment off Washington Square Park and a part-time job at the Whitney Museum of American Art. Amelia seemed to have contacts throughout NYC.

Blake introduced her to Sheldon, who became her acting

coach at $60 an hour – 'Lucky you know Amelia, kid – you're getting a bargain!' Sheldon taught her everything she needed to know about show business, as well as acting skills that took her to new heights. He fought to get her the roles of Signora Grimaldi and her two sisters. The play ran for two months at the Hudson Theatre on West 44th.

She turns the page:

> *New York Times, Theatre Review, October 2009. 'Jacqueline Donovitch, always known as Jax, an actress from Charlotte, North Carolina, excels in three different roles in an off-Broadway show. An Italian spoof: La Reincarnazione del Dottore Grimaldi.'*

Two years later came her last acting job in America. Playing the role of Sylvia was a real challenge – with many changes of make-up and clothes. The critics were kind:

> *CNN news coverage, June 2011. 'Donovitch – Jax – is heart-wrenching playing Sylvia, a widow three times Jax's own age. Rumour has it she's been offered a part in a play to be staged at the Adelphi, London.'*

She glances at her watch – 07.00am - and calls for a taxi on her iPhone: "Yeah, taxi for the Olympic Park, please ... right away." She stands and wanders over to the window to look out for her ride. Beneath the Georgian sash is an upright piano, its lid open. She plays a few notes that develop into 'Someone like you,' by Adele. Her vocal accompaniment is interrupted by the beep of a car horn in the street below. "Here we go again," she whispers to herself, "make or break."

Olympic Park

Stratford, London

Jax pads along the slip-resistant surface of a 10-metre-high diving platform. She has a strong, athletic figure, honed by the scrupulous self-discipline of demanding exercise: running, Pilates and yoga. Each sport keeps her in peak physical shape. But diving into water from a great height isn't for fun.

She comes to the end of the platform, takes a breath and feels that same old terror, a raw fear of water that challenges every sinew of her body and lies deep within her. She knows she must overcome those demons which no psychiatrist could rid her of.

She stares ahead and focuses, ignoring everything around her. Her breaths rise and fall and Jax knows her pulse is racing. It's always the same: apprehension and fear. The springs of the board creak as she stretches in preparation to dive, arching her back until her muscles protest..

Jax stares down at the pool, the water shimmering blue and dangerously far below her. She plunges headfirst, a perfect dive through the air and perforates the surface of the water. Jax swims desperately up to the top, gasps for air. Then she powers through the water, her face twisted with anguish. She reaches the side of the pool and stretches out towards her towel. She scrunches her eyes shut. Jagged images fill her mind: her mother's trong arms; blood; fear; and Bruno Kaminski's corpse.

She forces her mind back to the sound of her beloved Mozart, then hauls herself out of the water in one single movement and bends for the towel. She's panting with exertion as she dries. Finally, she looks up at the high board, her eyes shine, and her delicate features break into the faintest trace of a smile. Yes, she thinks to herself, I am free. Finally, I have conquered those demons; I am no longer afraid of the water and I can move on with my life.

She shivers, finishing drying herself, dresses and doesn't look back.

Savoy Hotel

Strand, London

JAX FIRST MET ANDREW FLOWER in the American Bar at the Savoy, a year after her final dive at Olympic Park. She was now playing the part she'd been offered at the Adelphi in the Strand. It was supposed to be a comedy, but it simply wasn't funny. A few members of the cast were going to the Savoy after second rehearsal for a drink. They'd asked Jax to join them. That drink changed her life.

Jax had found Andrew an attractive man back then. He was forty with sandy-brown hair going grey at the temples and a neatly-styled goatee beard. His hairline was receding and his complexion freckly, face lined around the eyes. He wore aviator-style glasses with a silver frame. He was dressed in a blue and red striped blazer and lightweight chinos. Blazers, she discovered later, were his signature outfit. And he possessed a dozen of them. He was eloquent and charming. As they both stood at the bar, waiting to be served, he introduced himself. Jax was wary at first, but he sounded and acted like a well-healed bachelor. And he was holding an empty champagne flute expectantly at the bar.

"Just bought an E-Type at Bonhams and paid way too much for it."

"How so? How come you paid too much for it?" Jax had asked innocently. This was another world to the one she inhabited, but she knew what an E-Type was.

"The auctioneer was damn skilful, and I was too bloody greedy is how so. They know how to play the room and the bidding just went north. My fault. No excuse." He paused and looked at her more closely, carefully assessing. "You're American?"

"Yeah." She laughed. "Long ago."

Flower raised his eyebrows to enquire whereabouts she was from.

"Charlotte, North Carolina."

"Let me get you a drink. Champagne alright? I've got a bottle of Bolly behind the bar. Just waiting for Franco to give me a re-fill. They're busy. Maybe the afternoon matinees have been chucked out." He laughed and she found the expression chucked out amusing.

"Sure," Jax had said casually. She'd never tasted champagne; never heard of 'Bolly.'

And so, the evening had developed from a random encounter.

She learned all about him – a subject he loved to talk about – in detail. He owned a meat processing plant in Norfolk and was basically 'a simple farmer.' He'd grinned self-deprecatingly, to show her he was a lot more than that. He'd raced classic cars at Goodwood and Le Mans. He'd skied the most challenging black slopes in Zermatt and Whistler and appeared to know everything about everything. From cooking the perfect omelette: 'seasoning is the secret' – to sailing his yacht from Cowes to Torquay: 'sailing single-handed takes balls, you know. And I'm not afraid to admit it.'

On the greatest motor racing driver who'd ever lived, Stirling Moss: 'oh there have been others, of course. Fangio, Nikki Lauder, Schumacher. But consider the 1955 Mille Miglia for sheer endurance – Brescia to Rome and back.'

Jax had never heard of Stirling Moss, but she would remember Mille Miglia. The two words were lodged in her mind.

On the perfect Bloody Mary: "Obviously Russian vodka; Stolichnaya, tomato juice, pepper, Worcestershire Sauce, a pinch of fleur de sel and celery. In chilled glasses."

"So that's it," Jax had asked more casually. She'd never heard of fleur de sel either.

"Oh no. A measure of Amontillado sherry makes all the difference. Darker than Fino, but lighter than Oloroso. Named after the Montilla region of Spain where the style originated."

"Really?"

Flower had touched his temple, very much in the know: "It features prominently in Edgar Allan Poe's 'Tales of Mystery and Imagination': 'The Cask of Amontillado', short story."

Of course, didn't everyone know that? She thought to herself.

*

The question of marriage had never been mentioned until a day at the Ascot races, when he unexpectedly produced a sapphire engagement ring and proposed to her. They had been standing by the open boot of his Bentley, sharing a Fortnum's picnic hamper and a bottle of champagne. The proposal had been almost casual, but his sincerity was clear. She'd been taken aback but had said 'yes.'

Andrew was older than Jax; but what did it matter? She could learn to love him even if it took time. One thing was for certain, she couldn't bear to end up like her mama: in a strange country; lonely, widowed, and poor.

They married at Churchman House Registry Office in Norwich. Christopher, Andrew's business partner, and confidant was best man. Their friend Lucia played the unofficial role of maid of honour. There was no prenuptial agreement or legal document for her to sign. Andrew preferred to keep the Flower Company in his name – 'for tax reasons' – and the decision made sense to Jax. She wasn't after Andrew's money; she was more relieved to have the comfort and security of a marriage. Andrew was happy for her to do more or less as she pleased: to be hostess for business luncheon meetings, give piano lessons to a few local children and run Brook House, the Flower family residence in Salhouse, Norfolk.

It seemed incredibly fortunate to her that she could be so lucky and that he felt the same way about her. After all the bad breaks in her life it was now time for her to have a few good ones.

Phone Call

The Flower Residence, Salhouse, Norfolk
Present day

BROOK HOUSE IS AN English country home. An elegant Grade two manor house with six-bedrooms, an interior swimming pool complex and a fine sweeping driveway leading to the front door of the house and garage. The driveway is often occupied by classic cars and today is no exception. A red Triumph TR4A sits on the drive with a bow around its bonnet and a bunch of helium-filled balloons hovering above it, bearing the number '5'.

Andrew Flower's late father, Raymond, had bought the property in the 1950s. It is not only luxurious but set within 5 acres of land and well away from the main Norwich Road. Raymond appreciated privacy then and so does Andrew now.

Andrew and Jax have now been married for five years and today is their wedding anniversary. The classic car is a gift from her to him. And she is not sure whether or not she has made the right decision. It is a surprise and Andrew normally relishes surprises. She looks around her very modern, well- equipped kitchen.

Her friend Lucia Paluzzi is sitting at the kitchen island – it was she who'd sold Jax the car – after months of trying to find just the right spec. Jax is agitated and preoccupied. The phone rings and she just knows it is her husband and that the call will be disappointing. Most of them have been, of late. As usual, there is no preamble: not a how are you? or how was your day? Andrew is straight in, but that was his manner. And in a way, it was what had attracted her in the first place. But that initial bluntness held no appeal to her now.

"Listen, I can't make dinner tonight, Jax. I'm sorry."

"Oh." She can't hide the disappointment. There is no mention of their wedding anniversary, or any endearments whatsoever.

Andrew Flower sits at his desk in his office, wearing factory overalls. And he isn't sorry at all. In front of him on the desk is his attaché case. It is stacked full of cash: Euros, Dollars, Sterling; a passport and various travel tickets.

"Oh," she says again with a deep swallow. "How so?"

"I have things to attend to here at the plant."

Jax says simply: "Shame."

"Yes, I know. But I've got to test run some machines for compliance. You know how it is, don't you?"

"Sure. I've gotten used to how it is, I guess." Even though Jax has lived in England for years she has retained her American accent. Jax looks across at Lucia who is nursing a generous glass of red wine from Tuscany. It is a gift from Lucia to the happy couple. In the event, she decided the car is enough expectation for one day and opened the bottle anyway.

Lucia, a fiery Sicilian brunette is very reminiscent of Italian actress, Monica Bellucci. She tries not to listen or react. She feels disappointed for her friend and raises her eyebrows.

Jax attempts persuasion: "Cannelloni? Homemade by Lucia, I gotta confess. Oh, but I found a very old bottle of Château Latour from that guy you know in Norwich. Tell me you're not tempted?" She switches to speakerphone so Lucia can hear the conversation.

Andrew tries his best to sound sincere: "Tempted, yes of course I am, darling, but committed too. I'll be just as quick as I can. You understand ... don't you? I, I have a deadline." He pauses for effect and can't help sounding patronising. "And we know deadlines can't wait, don't we, Jax?"

"Sure ... I'm just, uh. Call me when you're done ... okay? I'll come and get you."

He hesitates. Jax looks at Lucia, holds the receiver away from her face as if wanting to be dissociated with a lie.

"Y-Yes. Uh, maybe. I may decide to get a taxi later... especially if you've had a drink or two with Lucia."

"Sure."

Jax hangs up and wanders back to where Lucia sits at the kitchen island. She brushes away a tear and looks at Lucia for some sort of guidance.

Lucia sips her wine: "Oh ... that's too bad. He must work. On your wedding anniversary. I'd be mad as hell." Jax sits back down on the stool, slugs some wine.

"I am as mad as hell."

Lucia looks at her, grabs her car keys, glances at the door: "Tesoro. Bella. I must go. Andrew is so damn selfish, Jax. But I know what I'd do."

"Yeah, so do I."

Traffic

Norwich City Centre

FRIDAY NIGHT STREET SOUNDS and chaos: traffic, car horns, bright lights and noisy teenagers high on skunk. Jax is driving an Audi Q4 Sportback. On the passenger seat is her hamper: an insulated food box and beside it the precious bottle of Château Latour in a padded wine-bottle sleeve. At traffic lights, a group of youths suddenly slap the roof and bonnet, making offensive sexual gestures at her. Two of them try to rock the car. She hits the central locking and floors it, ignoring the red light.

Somebody hoots loudly at her in protest, and although it frightens her, she speeds off into the night, ignoring the irate motorist.

Blood Track

Flower Group Meat Processing Plant, Norwich

OUTSIDE THE PLANT, the Audi screeches to an abrupt stop. Jax struggles with her hamper and hurries to the main entrance. The door is unlocked, and she walks towards the automated production area. She glances up at a wall-mounted state-of-the-art digital control box.

CURRENT ALARM STATUS: DISARMED
CURRENT CCTV STATUS: OFF

Once inside she finds there is a tremendous, pulsating noise from the heavy-duty factory machinery. It's freezing. She hurries through the production area. Huge carcasses and slabs of meat hang on hooks above a static conveyor belt. She runs, colliding into carcass after carcass. She is utterly repelled by the smell of blood and dead meat.

She sees the familiar narrow steel staircase to a gantry above the conveyor belt. She waits, catches her breath and climbs the stairs onto the gantry. Once there she makes her way along the corridor towards her husband's office, not glancing over the rail. She is breathing rapidly, not thinking and yet completely focused, her mind on auto-pilot. She sees a sign indicating Andrew Flower's Office and hurries towards it. She nearly drops the hamper and wine sleeve but saves them at the last moment.

*

The office is unoccupied, but Andrew's desk is littered with papers, travel documents and his passport. A closed attaché case perches on the edge of the desk. The lock clasps are open. Jax pushes the hamper and wine sleeve onto the desk, making a space.

She notices the computer is on at the Lufthansa home page. She's curious: airline tickets, hotel vouchers. She picks them up, flicks through. Stena Line ferry tickets to Holland. She imitates Andrew's voice; the sound is uncanny:

"Happy anniversary, darling."

Suddenly the office door opens, and Andrew comes in. He looks completely surprised but tries hard not to show how shocked he is. Jax is startled and shouts out, her voice unnaturally high with shock:

"Shit! Andrew! You startled me! Boy!" She is still holding the bundle of travel documents, confused. He sees them, and is immediately alarmed:

"Jax! Are you alright? I – I thought I heard ... uh ..."

She tries to be dismissive: "Oh! Just a bunch of thugs at the traffic lights ...scared the shit out of me ... plus the smell out there makes me wanna puke."

He gives her a look of mock sincerity: "You get used to it, Jax. You have to." His tone implies the things he has to put up with in order to furnish her charmed life.

Jax agrees with a shrug: "I guess. Anyway, I've brought you a present."

Andrew's eyes dart to the hamper and wine sleeve: "A present?"

She opens the hamper and a plate wrapped in tin foil is revealed. She touches it: "Sure. I gotta confess it was Lucia's idea. And it's hot ...whoa!"

Andrew tries to smile, but it just won't work. He's too distracted:

"That's uh, great, Jax, but ..."

She closes the hamper and plucks the dusty old bottle out of the sleeve, weighing it in her hand: "Well, got a corkscrew? It won't open by itself."

Andrew walks further into the office, his eyes quickly darting from her face down to her hand. He sighs with impatience:

"Somewhere, yes ... I'll ..."

Jax is looking at the tickets as if they are suddenly starting to make sense. She continues: "Yeah ... 1982... very expensive; but hey, five years is five years, right? Special, huh?"

Andrew's tone is dripping sarcasm: "Yes, but you shouldn't have gone to so much trouble." He is mocking her, and she can't see it because she is more interested in the tickets now.

"It's ok... and maybe some glasses? Decent ones too. We can't drink this out of plastic water-fountain beakers."

Andrew ignores her: "Yes. What are you doing with those, Jax?"

"Do you know, I've never been to Miami? Or Amsterdam for that matter. Well, well." She pauses and thinks as if recalling a previous conversation she'd half-forgotten. "But wait, I thought you said Amsterdam was business?"

"Yes, I did."

She opens one of the airline tickets and sees:

LUFTHANSA FRANKFURT TO MIAMI,
BUSINESS CLASS, LH 462.
Name of Passenger: Elisabeth Deluc.

Jax looks up at him, genuinely puzzled.

"That's weird. Who the hell is Elisabeth Deluc?"

He raises his voice: "Please give them to me, Jax."

"What?" Her puzzlement turns to fear.

"I said give them to me. It's a perfectly clear instruction."

"Instruction?"

Andrew is serious and he moves in closer to her to retrieve them: "Yes, instruction."

Their eyes meet: "Andrew. Who is Elisabeth Deluc?"

"Give them to me." He holds his hand out now, jabbing his open palm at her, moving closer. He suddenly shouts: "Now!"

"Andrew, stop this. You're frightening me. I can't deal ..." Jax glances down at the ticket. In that split-second, he flips and makes a grab for them.

He snarls: “You want me to spell it out?”

“Yeah, I do.”

“What do you think? I’ve met somebody.”

“Since when?”

“A year. Now give me those bloody tickets.”

Jax is incredulous: “You’ve been seeing someone a year? Another woman? A year? Jesus.”

She starts to move back and continues: “So, when were you planning to tell me, huh?”

“Tonight. Now give them to me. Or I’ll take them from you.”

She is still moving back because she can see he is deadly serious: “Tonight?” She dances quickly around the edge of the desk, feeling her way blindly behind her with her empty hand. He is onto her now. She’s not going to get away. Her fear is palpable. The closed attaché case is still perched on the edge of the desk. As she sidles around, she knocks into it. It falls. And for a moment they both stare at it, wondering what will happen next.

Bundles of banknotes spill out from it: Euros, Dollars, Pounds. She stares down at the money with confusion and growing terror. As she looks back at him, he slaps her across the face with the back of his hand. Dazed, she drops the tickets. She’s shocked and touches her bloody mouth.

“Damn fucking Lucia with her crazy ...” His eyes catch sight of the wine bottle: A possible weapon.

Jax tears out of the office, running for her life along the corridor. Behind her now, he is also running towards the gantry.

*

They are both on the gantry now above 'the blood track' where carcasses are sent for disposal. The track consists of rows of now empty hooks above a static conveyor belt - weight activated - which leads onto the meat pulveriser and incinerator.

Andrew shouts, too crazy now to register reality: "Let's try and talk."

She looks over the railing, wiping her bloody lip: "Really?" A glance over her shoulder. He is ten feet behind her now and getting closer. She grips the rail, terrified, sure he will kill her; she tries to stall. He slows to a walking pace directly towards her.

She plays for time: "How could you do that to me, Andrew?"

"People change."

"Yeah, I guess they do. And to think I bought you a classic car for our anniversary."

"Oh, yes? With what, exactly?"

"Money, what do you think?"

A trickle of venom: "But whose money?"

Jax sighs: "Mine."

"Mine, I think. It's all mine. You don't have a bean."

"I do! It was money which I'd saved, from my mother's estate."

"A couple of lousy dollars from that no good polski uchodźca."

"What the hell did you call my mother?"

"I think you heard."

Jax is incredulous.

His spite is raw: "The money is mine. You contribute nothing. You can't even give me children." He is in front of her now, right in her face. And she screams at him.

"Yes, and you know why I can't. That pig Kaminski raped me and tore my insides."

"So what? I knew. Maybe you led him on, God knows what you were like back then." His comment is cruel.

"How can you say that?"

He swings at her face again; starts to lose his balance. It's happening fast. The momentum of his punch. He plunges forward over the guard rail onto 'the blood track' below. The impact of his weight automatically triggers the conveyor bel system to activate.

He's either unconscious or dead.

His body is dragged onto an enclosed mincer of steel worms and blades. They are sharp enough to pulverise and chop bone into mush for waste disposal into the incinerator. It takes seconds. In a few more minutes the remains will be ashes. Jax is on her knees, looking down at the bloody conveyor belt. Exhausted she rolls over onto her side, curls up into a ball and cries.

His words echo: 'You can't even give me children.' She gasps for breath; her body is shaking as she sobs. Suddenly she stands and runs to the washroom.

*

Once inside, she's violently sick into the basin. She turns on the cold tap – full blast – rinsing her mouth out, splashing water onto her face. She stares at her face in the mirror, shaking with fear, dabbing her bloody lips with a paper towel. She looks at her eyes – dilated pupils – the black centres so much larger than normal: raw emotion. Her teeth start to chatter and then she sees something in reflection: Andrew's jacket on a coat hanger. For a second it looks like a person. She screams, and swings round and sees what it is. Relieved, she walks towards it. She taps the pockets and takes out his wallet and iPhone.

Suddenly the silence is broken by a familiar ringtone: the sound of a Formula One engine. The shock of the interruption startles her. Still shaking, she drops the phone but catches it, staring at the screen she sees:

Elisabeth 0049 30 895584.

She panics, switches the phone off and opens the door of the washroom. The wallet and iPhone she jams into her pocket. She walks down the corridor towards Andrew's office, dabbing her bloody lip with a tissue.

*

Once back in the office she sees the attaché case. The dropped tickets. The key fob to the Audi. The money. She walks around the desk and very slowly picks up the telephone receiver. Her finger hovers over '9', hesitates for a second, then she slams it down.

She picks up the tickets, sifts through them. Her hands are

shaking. She gathers all the documents from the desk, picks up the attaché case, and replaces all the spilled cash. She puts the passport, air and ferry tickets into it. Picks up the car key fob. Next, she takes the hamper, the wine sleeve, attaché case and places them outside the office door. She pauses. She takes a napkin out of the food box and methodically wipes down all the surfaces she has touched. It's as if she is on auto-pilot. She goes down, under the gantry, to the conveyor belt where Andrew had fallen. She takes a pressure hose and sprays down the whole area. She's gagging; a final glance around to make sure she's forgotten nothing. She returns to Andrew's office to retrieve the attaché and other items she'd left out in the corridor.

*

At the front door, she takes the master key card from Andrew's wallet. At that moment, the door opens, and Mick, the factory foreman walks in. He's a local man of sixty who has been a loyal employee of the Flower company since he started his apprenticeship as a slaughterman.

His jovial expression turns to concern as he sees Jax: "Mrs Flower! What happened? Are you alright?"

Jax, caught off-guard, touches her lip: "Mick? Oh? I slipped over just now. I'm collecting my husband. I'm – I'm fine ... thanks. Where've you been then?" She can't help but notice the blood-stained overalls.

"King's Lynn, collecting a load of contaminated carcasses for tomorrow's first run. Six o'clock start."

She grimaces at the thought: "Oh, I see."

Mick looks puzzled: "Where is Mr Flower?"

"Out in the car, waiting for me, I hope. Special day." She points with her chin at the car park.

Mick walks closer, stares at her: "Didn't notice him. Saw the Audi though, parked up in his space ... are you sure you don't need the First Aid Kit?"

"No, thanks. It looks worse than it is. Oh well, maybe Andrew's gone to buy me a bouquet of roses. It's our anniversary, you see." She doesn't have to explain, it's none of his business, but she does anyway. Her nerves are doing the talking.

Mick eyes the attaché case and other items. She conceals the master key card and continues in her happy-go-lucky way: "Must run. Leave you to shut up shop as usual. I'll check the Tesco Express, huh? He's probably there chatting up the assistants. Have a good evening."

Mick nods knowingly: "He'd be better off at Mousehold Garden Centre. Better selection of roses there. And assistants."

"Yeah, I get it, Mick." Jax turns and runs towards the car, calling her husband's name into the empty darkness.

Mick watches her walking towards the Audi. He's heard rumours over the years about Andrew's infidelity. He's always dismissed such idle gossip: who'd want to cheat on a woman like Jacqueline? She's a lovely person, always animated and cheerful towards factory employees. He'd heard her play the piano and sing at Christmas parties for the staff's children. She sounds like Adele, or was it someone else? Whoever it was, she sounded the part.

Brook House

The Flower Residence, Salhouse, Norfolk

THE SWEEPING DRIVEWAY to the house is pitch black as the Audi approaches it. And then the security lights flick on. The drive and the house are illuminated like a film set. The classic Triumph TR4A sports car sits on the drive, like a prize exhibit at a motor show. A downpour has caused the red bow to slip off the bonnet down to the ground, the balloons are deflated.

Jax pulls up outside the front door and the car stops. She grips the wheel, looking at the Triumph, its celebratory decorations abandoned in the rain. It seems to encapsulate how she feels. Finally, she sighs, gets out and hurries to the front door.

*

Jax enters the hallway clutching the hamper, wine sleeve and attaché case. She moves into the kitchen, puts all the items on the counter. She opens the attaché case, stares at the contents once again. Disbelief. She takes the bundles of cash, stuffs them into a carrier bag and puts it into a cupboard under the kitchen sink. Her hands are shaking.

Then she returns to the attaché case again. She sees the business class air ticket to Miami, passenger name Elisabeth Deluc. She fixes herself her customary drink: a large Jack Daniel's on the rocks. She downs a generous slug; she's trembling and staring at the phone. She grabs it, punches some numbers, and waits.

"Lu! Thank God! Please get over here right away!"

Lucia sounds sleepy: "What's going on?"

"Andrew's . . . dead."

"What?"

For a moment Jax hesitates, not sure, scared.

Her friend continues: "Jax? How?"

"Please just come over."

"Give me ten minutes." Lucia hangs up abruptly.

"Door's open."

*

Jax waits at the window, sipping her JD. She sees Lucia's VW Karmann Ghia pull onto the driveway, and she sobs with relief. Lucia gets out of the car and lets herself in. She comes into the kitchen and hugs her friend. Jax explains, between sobs, exactly what happened at the plant. She is totally distraught. Lucia is composed, listening. She slowly pulls away from the embrace and looks Jax in the eye.

"Why didn't you call the police?"

Jax whispers: "I don't know. I don't ... I didn't kill him, Lu. I swear. I wouldn't lie to you ... please believe me ... it was an accident." She pauses awkwardly.

"Yes, you said so. I understand."

Slowly, Lucia picks up items from Andrew's attaché case: hotel vouchers, Stena ferry tickets to Holland.

She studies the airline ticket:

LUFTHANSA FRANKFURT TO MIAMI

BUSINESS CLASS, LH 462.

Name of passenger: Elisabeth Deluc.

She sighs: "Who stands to gain from Andrew's death?" It's an obvious question and one Jax has never even considered.

"Me, I guess. Andrew has no other family. Unless he changed his will. He may have changed it if he was planning to leave me ..." Jax is speaking her thoughts out loud. Lucia interrupts her:

"This is evidence, Jax. Against you. It gives you a motive."

"But I didn't kill him, Lu. I promise ... oh my God."

Lucia shakes her head: "Says who, Jax? Who? Any CCTV there?

"Yeah – switched off. Andrew must have switched it off because of what he was doing ... I don't know ..." She sobs again.

"Listen. You didn't call the police. Some of your fingerprints must be there. Your being there - finding out about his sordid affair – is enough. You ran. And that man Mick is a potential witness. Can't you see? Any jury would nail you." Lucia waits.

"But he swung at me. The momentum carried him over the rail."

"Si … but how can you prove it?"

Jax shakes her head: "They'll – they'll believe me. They will." She picks up the phone to call the police.

Lucia dashes round the kitchen island and grabs Jax's shoulders: "Look at me."

Her eyes are red and bloodshot, her make-up has run, her lip is cut and swollen. But she listens.

"You can't call them. Not now."

"But I must, Lucia. I must."

"Just think a minute, Jax … you didn't call them right away. Think of your mother. They'll find out about her and use it against you. The lawyers will twist this."

"No, surely they'll believe me?" Her head slumps forward and she remembers that night in Lafayette. The quaint, old American bathroom. "My God, Lu …."

*

Jax recounts that night in vivid detail, describing events as they unfolded: she's in the bathtub; tendrils of wispy steam hang in the room; out of nowhere the shadow of a man softly creeps in. It is her uncle, Bruno Kaminski.

"Smells sweet in here, honey." Still the heavy Eastern European accent, slurred with drink.

Jax gulps: "What do you want, Uncle Bruno?"

A drunken laugh: "You know what I want, and I want it again." The footfalls advance in the swirling mist; the sound of a working man's boots, tough leather squeaking.

Jax says: "Go away. You shouldn't be here." Kaminski kneels, his hand is in the water, exploring, trying to touch her. She struggles to push him away and the water sloshes over the side of the bath. Kaminski is laughing, anticipating, wanting.

She screams: “No! Don’t. No!”

But Kaminski won’t give up; he’s hungry for her.

She screams again, an ear-piercing shriek: “Mama!”

More sloshing water as she tries to stand up, but it’s useless. He’s strong and she struggles for her life. She screams for her mother again.

Kaminski belches: “Ain’t no use screamin’, Jax. Your precious mama is as drunk as a skunk. You think I didn’t see to that?”

Jax crashes back down into the bath, defeated. Through the mist she catches sight of the large old bathroom mirror. In the reflection, she sees a figure silently step into the room, gripping an old golf iron. Cautiously, the figure advances. Jax continues to struggle against Kaminski in the mist. The foamy bathwater slops noisily over the side of the tub. His breathing is heavy with exertion and alcohol. He senses he is near to getting what he came for again ...

Behind, the figure swings the golf iron and catches the side of Kaminski’s skull. A cascade of blood hits the mirror as he spins down to the floor. Jax’s mother smiles grimly at the body.

“Except I didn’t drink your poisoned hooch, Kaminski. You son of a bitch.”

Jax is screaming.

“Come here Jax, baby ... You’re okay. I’m here now. It’s okay ... Hold me tight ... He won’t touch you no more, baby. But I had to see for myself, Jax. Just what a monster Bruno really was. I'm sorry. I should have believed you."

*

Jax is in pieces now. Lucia is shocked; she's never heard the story before in such detail. Jax recalls the New Orleans newspaper headline: "Mother convicted. Second-degree murder. On death row.'

Jax turns to Lucia: "But she killed Kaminski to save me, Lu."

"Bella! So, you did what you learned from your mom. That's what some smart-ass barrister is going to make a jury believe. And they will. They will want to believe it because that's the way people are."

Jax's reply is a whisper: "No. It's how it was."

"Your word against some very smart lawyer, Jax. And you stand to gain a fortune, let's face it."

"No. We don't know that."

"Jax, do you really want to take that risk?"

Jax is panting, exhausted, drained. Drops to the kitchen floor. Lucia kneels, takes the phone from her and places it back on the cradle. She takes her hand: "You can't go to the police and tell them what really happened this evening."

"Then what am I going to do?"

"I am your friend, I'll help you. Phone them but just report him as missing. Buy some time."

"I'm not sure, Lu."

Lucia risks a chuckle: "I am absolutely sure. But don't call them until Monday. I'm certain you'll think of something."

Dressing Room

Brook House, Salhouse, Norfolk

JAX SITS IN THE DRESSING ROOM, in her bathrobe; her hair is wrapped up in a towel like a turban, the way she always does. She's holding Andrew's passport in her hand and staring at the photograph. She is lost in thought. She looks up at her collection of framed film posters: Mrs Doubtfire; Sliding Doors; Tootsie. The seed of an idea is sprouting.

She stands up and goes over to her open-plan wardrobe and a massive collection of clothes. There are assorted wigs on mannequin heads. She takes her old suitcase out and opens it. Inside there is a catalogue: *KYROLAN PROFESSIONAL MAKE-UP* for theatre, film and television.

She wanders over to a circular make-up mirror and sits down. She puts on a pair of Andrew's aviator-style glasses. Tilted against the jar of solvent is a photograph of Andrew – full face. There is a plastic palette of stipple wax, a blusher brush, crêpe hair particles, mastix spirit gum to stick down the beard, crêpe hair for the eyebrows and a latex nose that will totally alter the shape of her face.

Forty minutes later she looks at herself in the make-up mirror to check the makeover: Andrew's neatly styled goatee beard, sandy-brown hair and freckly complexion are perfectly captured.

Tempted, yes of course I am, darling, but committed too ... you understand ... don't you? I have a deadline ... The voice is not quite right, but it will be. After all, Jax has a deadline too.

Biltmore Hotel

Coral Gables, Miami, Florida, USA.

HIS VIEW OF THE GOLF COURSE is spectacular. Juan de Pablos (Jnr) is twenty-five years old. He sits at a table on the veranda of his suite at the Biltmore and admires the vast green course under a deep-blue sky. He's Hispanic, handsome, dressed in J. Lindeberg designer golf attire. He holds a hotel landline phone to his ear.

His voice is mellifluous and accentless: "Yes, and my father is in hospital here in Miami. He is having renal dialysis. Where is Mr Andrew Flower?"

The voice at the other end belongs to Christopher Fielding, Flower's business partner at the meat processing plant in Norwich: "Holland. As in the Netherlands."

"I know where the Netherlands are, Mr Fielding. I've tried his mobile. No response." De Pablos's tone is now one of frustration and annoyance.

"Oh. Oh. Did you leave Andrew a message?"

"No."

Fielding says nothing; it is wiser, he feels, to let the other man do the talking. Which he does in no uncertain terms. There is a flavour of menace:

"The contract is here, Mr Fielding. You have our money in your account. A great deal of it. We are not a family who waits. And we do not leave messages. You are sellers and we are the buyers. We hold the upper hand. Is that clear?"

Before Fielding can reply the phone has been slammed down in Miami.

Conference Room

Flower Group, Norwich

IT'S MONDAY, AND CHRISTOPHER FIELDING is miffed. He's early-forties and well-coiffed: clean-shaven, dressed in a button-down Oxford shirt and grey flannels. His ex-mother-in-law, the redoubtable Delta McQueen QC, described him as a boulevardier. In other words, he was the epitome of a wealthy, fashionable socialite. Dapper and very well-connected. Fielding is equally at home in the Burlington Arcade or on the fairway at Sunningdale. His permanent tan is testament to his devotion to sunshine and fresh air: sailing on the Norfolk Broads, hiking in Scotland and skiing three times each season. He runs his fingers through a lock of silver-grey hair and sighs irritably ...

He's just put the phone down from his conversation with Juan de Pablos, still piqued at the abrupt way the call was terminated. And de Pablos's superior attitude.

Fielding's law degree has stood him in good stead as Andrew Flowers's business partner and confidant. He has made a great deal of money in property speculation and will make a lot more if current negotiations with de Pablos proceed according to plan.

He picks up the phone again, calls a mobile number from memory. It switches to answerphone, and he curses, but leaves a message anyway: "Andrew, I'm sorry we didn't speak last night. My tennis match overran dreadfully ... at least we won. I assume you are en route to Amsterdam. Call me, please." He pauses for a moment as if checking his busy schedule. "Mobile is best. Or at the Rectory after seven. I'll be in."

Fielding wipes his brow. He always calls his eight-bedroom home in North Norfolk the Rectory, yet it is nowhere near a church. His ex-wife Nina called the affectation pretentious, kinder than many of the adjectives Delta used to describe his character.

Ferry

Harwich International Ferry Port, Essex.

LATER THAT SAME MONDAY, it is dark outside as Andrew Flower's Audi Q4 pulls up alongside the booth. The Stena Line attendant waits to check travel documents for the 2300hr crossing over to Holland.

"Good evening, sir. Tickets and passport, please."

With gloved hands, Jax passes the assorted documents over as the car is checked in. The man seems to take forever checking the booking and consulting his computer. Her anxiety makes the procedure seem longer than it really is.

"Thank you, Mr Flower. . . plenty of time ... you're not travelling with any pets on this voyage this evening? ... They all have to be checked in now."

"No pets. Just me."

He hands the documents back to her: "OK, you're all checked in. Lane three please, then through to ship side. Departure is in about twenty-five minutes. Just follow the others."

"Thank you." She edges the car forwards towards UK Border

Security and the queue of cars waiting to board the Stena Hollandica for Holland. A border guard looks the car over and briefly underneath, then waves her on.

Holland

Stena Line Ferry Port Arrivals, Hoek van Holland

EARLY THE FOLLOWING morning, the Audi rolls down the ramp onto the quayside and joins the queue of other cars arriving in Holland. Jax looks through Andrew's glasses and her vision is slightly out of focus. She's cautious, not wanting to draw attention. At Passport Control she slows down and hands the passport across to the attendant. After a brief computer check, it is stamped HOEK VAN HOLLAND/EUROPOORT H028 and dated.

She pulls away with a sigh of relief and heads up towards the big roundabout and eventually joins the A4 to Amsterdam. The Satnav tells her it is 83km and will take her 1hr 7mins. She stretches back in the seat and tries to relax for the journey..

*

Jax pulls into a lay-by and takes Andrew's iPhone out of the attaché case. There has been one missed call and one message.

1 – 305 – 445 – 1926 (missed call/DePablos)

01603 757575 (message/Fielding.)

She makes a mental note of the two calls and, after a moment, pulls back onto the main road and flicks on the radio. It immediately seeks 101.9 FM, and she sings along to classic rock and pop. Now she's ready.

Hotel De L'europe

Nieuwe Doelenstraat, Amsterdam, Holland.

JAX PARKS THE AUDI outside the hotel, enters the lobby and walks to reception carrying Andrew's attaché case and a suitcase. A uniformed concierge nods to her, but she shakes her head; no help needed. He can see she's in a dreadful rush for an important meeting. The reservations clerk greets her and asks how she may help. Jax looks the part and she's straight in:

"Hello. My friend has booked and confirmed a suite for us through Leading Hotels of the World. You sent her a payment link and she has already settled the bill on-line. Two nights. Her name is Jacqueline Donovitch."

The reservations clerk taps away on her computer: "Ah yes, sir. I see her booking is confirmed and paid for."

"May I leave my suitcase here, please – I have a medical conference at the AMC – also this attaché case must be kept somewhere secure."

"Yes, I'll have the suitcase sent up to your suite and the attaché case put in our client safe."

“That’s very kind.” Jax glances at Andrew’s Rolex. “I must dash. Miss Donovitch will check in later when she comes in from Schiphol.”

“Yes, of course. As the room is paid for, I can give you a key card, a very nice canal- facing suite on the second floor.” The clerk presents the key card in a paper wallet.

Jax hesitates: “Don’t need it now, but yes, alright. It makes sense in case she is held up. Thanks.”

*

She dashes back out to the car and the Satnav takes her to a cavernous underground car park on Beurs Plein near Warmoesstraat. She walks up the steep ramp of the car park out into daylight, holding an Amsterdam street map. She is now carrying Andrew’s Louis Vuitton suitcase and matching suit carrier. Gravenstraat is a main thoroughfare in the centre of the city.

Dam Square Inn

Gravenstraat, Amsterdam, Holland.

AT THE SECOND HOTEL, the reservations clerk is a Dutch girl called Anna Brun. She says good evening as Jax hands her a printed e-mail:

"Hello. Flower Group in Norwich, England have booked and paid for a room. Three nights. Here is the confirmation. And my passport ..." Jax holds out Andrew's open passport, which Anna barely looks at.

"That's fine, Mr Flower, thank you." Anna hands the room key across. "No need to photocopy your passport, I can see from my screen we already hold your details on record. Your room is ready for you now. Do you need a hand with your luggage?"

"No. I'll manage." Jax turns towards the lift. "But thanks anyway."

*

The Dam Square Inn's entrance is actually on a narrow thoroughfare called Gravenstraat. And, outside it, a twenty-something man has been watching. He is holding a photograph of Andrew Flower and witnesses his arrival at the inn. Flower looks about forty, with sandy-brown hair going grey at the temples and a neatly-styled goatee beard. He wears aviator-style glasses with a silver frame. The blue and red striped blazer and lightweight chinos give the impression of understated elegance. The man takes out a mobile phone to report in, while walking towards a Dutch coffee shop. There is a large image of a hashish pipe on the window.

*

Jax leaves the Inn, walks up Gravenstraat to Nieuwezijds Voorburgwal and crosses the road to the Hotel Die Port van Cleve. The streetside restaurant is called Hulscher's, Amsterdam 1870. She is carrying her own overnight bag. Everything is in the correct place, ready for the next phase of her plan.

Hotel Die Port Van Cleve

Nieuwezijds Voorburgwal, Amsterdam

HULSCHER'S HAS THE FEEL of a traditional continental brasserie, with an open-plan and highly visible kitchen to the left. The restaurant is busy with diners: locals, tourists, businesspeople, and the odd family. Jax is shown to a previously booked table and studies the menu and wine list. After a few minutes she signals to the waiter who approaches with an order pad. She orders without preamble:

"I'd like the Dutch herring, but with no raw onions or gherkins; just French fries, please. And a bottle of Saracosa Governo Rosso."

The waiter scribbles the order with a very cheerful – bedankt – impressed with her choice of the 2020 red wine from Tuscany. After five minutes he reappears, carrying the bottle of wine and holds it at an angle so she can inspect the label. She nods and looks at him:

"I've left my mobile phone in my hotel room." She points across the street; the waiter nods as she stands. "Would you please put my order on hold for ten minutes. I need to get it."

She puts Andrew's gold credit card and two fifty Euro notes under the place mat, looks at him: "But open the wine, please. Let it air."

The waiter nods in understanding as she leaves the restaurant. She doesn't see him walk to the cash desk holding the credit card and tip – but she knows he will – and it is a moment he will remember. She doesn't see him walk to her booth and open the wine, smell the cork and pour her a soupçon into a wine glass.

But she knows he will.

*

Jax turns right out of Hulscher's and walks up towards Magna Platza, a shopping mall that was the former Amsterdam main post office. She is still carrying her overnight bag.

Across the street 'mobile-phone man' sees Jax leave the restaurant. He follows. She doesn't see him.

*

Jax hurries towards a taxi rank on Damrak. A taxi is waiting, she gets in, clutching her bag.

"Central station, please."

"No problem, sir," says the driver looking in his rear-view mirror, clicking the central locking.

She is dropped outside the station a few minutes later. She goes inside, waits ten minutes in the kiosk to kill time. It is a precaution she has considered all day and she doesn't know why. Except assume the worst. Who does Andrew know in Amsterdam? Is there any chance he would have been followed or watched? She hopes so; it might add to the illusion she has created.

She goes into a disabled cubicle, opens her overnight bag, takes out a dress and scarf and hangs them on a hook behind the door. She then takes off the aviator-style glasses, carefully removes the wig, peels off the goatee beard, latex nose and the crêpe hair that formed the eyebrows. She changes out of Andrew's blazer and chinos, folds them and places them carefully into her overnight bag. She unzips a side section and removes a sponge bag containing her feminine make-up. At the washbasin she uses solvent to clean off the spirit gum, foundation, and loose pieces of prosthetic. In a few moments the face that stares back at her is Jax. She applies a touch of make-up and lipstick, smooths down her dress and glances into the mirror to check her appearance: it has taken her ten minutes to swap identities.

She goes back outside and gets into another taxi: "Hôtel de L'Europe, please."

Discovery

Hôtel de L'Europe,
Nieuwe Doelenstraat, Amsterdam, Holland

JAX WALKS INTO THE LOBBY of the hotel and makes her way to reception. A reservations clerk greets her and asks how she may help.

"Hi, Jacqueline Donovitch. I have a reservation booked through Leading Hotels of the World." Jax shows her American passport which the clerk checks with the computer booking.

"That's fine, Miss Donovitch. And I have a note here on my screen that we are holding an attaché case here in our safe. Shall I have the concierge bring it up to your suite? It's in the client safe downstairs at the moment."

"Thank you, yes." Jax takes the proffered key card from the clerk and makes her way to the lift.

*

In her hotel suite, Jax fixes herself a Jack Daniels and ice from the minibar and lies back on the King Size bed, finally able to relax. The open attaché case is perched on top of the duvet and, as she makes herself comfortable, it tips back. And something catches her eye: a section sealed by Velcro she had not noticed before. She searches inside it and finds a soft-leather folder, the size of a paperback. She opens it and sees a private bank statement:

ABN AMRO PRIVATE BANKING. GUSTAV MAHLERLAAN 10, 1082 PP,AMSTERDAM, NETHERLANDS. Privilege Account Number 0272682368.

Mr Andrew Flower/Mr Christopher Fielding Current balance: £10,000,075 (Ten Million Pounds sterling.) Money transfer from Señor Juan de Pablos

Jax sips her JD and quietly absorbs the information. She had absolutely no clue this account ever existed. She feels sick in the pit of her stomach as she opens the second document from the soft-leather folder:

'CONTRACT BETWEEN THE FLOWER GROUP LTD (NORWICH) GREAT BRITAIN AND DE PABLOS CORPORATION (MIAMI) USA. '

'The contract between these two parties creates mutual obligations that are enforceable by law to acquire the company for which 10% has already been paid to ABN AMRO, Amsterdam. The contract includes the Flower Group meat processing plant in Norwich plus all outbuildings, refrigerated units and storage facilities. '
'This contract also includes the property known as BROOK HOUSE, Salhouse, Norfolk, England. The house will be auctioned once the acquisition takes place. Note: Mrs Jacqueline Flower is not party to the transactions and is not a beneficiary as she is not a shareholder of the company.'

Her head slumps back onto the stack of pillows as she realises the enormity of what she's read. She'd had no inkling he was selling the company; except his recent aloofness had mystified her until now. Now a lot of things are starting to make sense to her. And this Juan de Pablos – whoever he is – will take possession of her home on completion.

She feels wretched and violated. Everything she believed about Andrew and their future together has been a lie. He's cheated her out of everything, the ultimate betrayal. Lucia is the one person she can trust to see her through.

Mobile Phone Man

Damrak, Amsterdam, Holland

DAMRAK IS AN AVENUE and partially filled-in canal; the main route from the station to Dam Square. 'Mobile-phone man' is standing right in the middle of it looking around at the crowds: tourists, commuters, locals on bicycles. He looks completely stoned on Dutch skunk, his eyes red-rimmed and bleary. He taps out a number and speaks German:

"Flower left Die Port van Cleve restaurant and vanished, Fräulein. Yes, I'm sorry to say I've lost him ..." The voice at the other end is furious. So much so that he holds the phone away from his ear before saying again: "Yes, I've looked everywhere, Fräulein. There is no sign of him ... I will ..."

The line goes dead.

Motorcycle

Roland de Groot,
Motorcycle Dealer, Amsterdam, Holland

THE FOLLOWING MORNING, Jax emerges from the motorcycle showroom. She is wearing one-piece motorcycle leathers, balaclava, and wraparound sunglasses.

A mechanic rides her newly acquired Yamaha 125cc motorbike round from the workshop to the front of the building. She thanks the man, puts on a crash helmet, gets on the bike and rides it apprehensively along the cobbled streets around Waterlooplein. She makes her way back to the Hôtel de L'Europe, parks it outside and dismounts awkwardly.

*

Once inside her suite at the hotel, Jax transfers the soft leather folder with the two documents and travel tickets from the attaché case to one of two leather stuff sacks she'd bought from de Groot. Into the other she packs her clean clothes from her suitcase.

She pushes the empty attaché case under the bed and stows her now redundant Louis Vuitton suitcase in the wardrobe. She puts her Donovitch American passport into a pocket of her leathers and taps it reassuringly. Finally, she scans the room, picks up the two stuff sacks and leaves.

*

Jax leaves the Hôtel de L'Europe after depositing the two key cards at reception and walks down a cobbled street beside the Amstel. She takes out the Audi key fob and drops it discreetly into the river. There is a distinct 'plop' sound; and she watches as it sinks. For her this is a significant moment.

Once back outside the de L'Europe, she pushes the two stuff sacks into the motorcycle panniers and starts the engine hesitantly. She rides the motorcycle out of the city centre and joins the A10 ring road towards Schiphol airport.

Schiphol

Schiphol Airport, Amsterdam, Holland

AT DEPARTURES, JAX IS WATCHING. At her feet is the stuff sack with all of the items from Andrew's attaché case: the evidence of his betrayal.

She can see the Lufthansa check-in counter. A few people are queuing: Lufthansa flight Schiphol via Frankfurt to Miami. Jax has one of the tickets in her hand now and is cross- checking the flight details.

And then she sees a woman looking around, glancing at her watch anxiously. Jax figures it must be Elisabeth Deluc: right time, right place, right face. The sort of woman who would, no doubt, have appealed to Andrew. Jax's initial impression is that she looks Scandinavian: a tall curvaceous figure, well-defined jawline, high cheekbones. Her wavy blonde hair tumbles to the shoulders of a Ted Baker leather jacket. She wears a pair of tight-fitting jeans which cling to her like a second skin. She moves with graceful economy but is clearly distracted. The woman is anxiously making enquiries to one of the check-in clerks. The clerk shakes her head, tapping keys, checking the flight manifest on her computer screen. Definitely no one has already checked in with that name and ticket number.

The woman scans the crowd of passengers with growing annoyance. Her face says something's not right: departure looms and no Andrew Flower. What can be wrong?

*

At the Lufthansa check-in desk 'mobile-phone man' suddenly appears. He looks flushed, obviously late. He approaches the woman whose expression is grim. There is no greeting, no nicety at all. She speaks in rapid German:

"What the hell happened last night? You were supposed to watch Andrew Flower. How difficult can it possibly be?"

The man's tone is fraught with guilt: "I told you, he vanished. It was dark and crowded, Fräulein."

The woman shoots him a look; raises her hands in protest: "Stop. Ok? No more excuses."

"Ok." The man can't look at her, tries to change the subject: "I see your colleague is here, Fräulein. As you organised."

She sighs with exasperation: "Of course Griffiths is here, yes. But it's hardly relevant if Flower fails to show. Is it?"

She is watching the passengers very carefully: "Where can he be?" She checks her phone and they both search the sea of passengers around the check-in desks, looking for Andrew. The check-in clerk suddenly calls her, anxious and concerned.

"Miss Deluc! Miss Deluc!"

Elisabeth turns and acknowledges the call, with a polite 'yes' in English.

"We are closing the flight now. Do you want to check in? This is the last moment."

Elisabeth cools a degree: "No, no thank you. Thank you for your help and patience." She switches briefly to Dutch out of courtesy: "Heel erg bedankt." Thank you very much.

The Dutch girl smiles as the woman pulls out her phone, scrolls through her contacts and calls a mobile phone number.

Vantage Point

Schiphol Departures, Holland

JAX IS SIMULTANEOUSLY WATCHING the events unfold from a discreet distance and hears the check-in clerk address Miss Deluc by name. So, from this point on Jax definitely knows the identity of the woman called "Elisabeth." But she doesn't know what has just been said between her and 'mobile-phone man'. Jax sees her still pacing around, looking and searching for Flower among the hordes of departing passengers.

Jax sees Elisabeth take out her phone and make a call.

*

Andrew's phone suddenly roars into life in Jax's pocket. The Formula One Engine ringtone is completely unexpected. She struggles to get it out of the pocket of her leathers where it has become jammed. Finally, it's out and she stares at the screen in amazement.

ELISABETH: 0049 30 895584

Jax can't help but smile, despite the shock. Her rival is over there, confused. She switches the phone off and stuffs it back in her pocket. She needs to get back on the road.

*

Up in the elevated concourse of airport Departures, Hywel Griffiths, HMRC tax inspector, has witnessed events with curiosity. Griffiths is a former soldier from Grangetown, Cardiff. Twelve years' service with Royal Signals had given him the opportunity to escape from poverty, but it had also instilled in him a sense of bitterness against people with money.

Griffiths thoroughly resented inherited wealth, or what he considered was 'undeserved.' He was naturally astute with numbers; unmarried and obsessed with work. Griffiths thinks of himself as a detective, with financial skills which confound his colleagues.

From his vantage point, Griffiths hears the distinctive sound of Andrew's iPhone. He immediately becomes suspicious when both Elisabeth and the leather-clad biker hang up at the same time. What's going on? Who is the figure in motorcycle leathers?

*

Back at the Lufthansa check-in desk, Elisabeth, both frustrated and annoyed, is still looking around. She turns to 'mobile-phone man': "He's not going to show. Come on, let's get back to base."

"Ja, Fräulein."

Elisabeth makes another call, but is transferred to answerphone: "Herr Wagner? It's Elisabeth. Flower's a no-show. I have no idea what happened. We'll speak soon – I'll call you if there is an update."

*

Jax emerges from her discreet corner and dashes to the P1 Short-term parking on Ceintuubaan Zuid and pays using her phone.

*

From the elevated concourse, Griffiths watches like a hawk. The image of a woman in full motorcycle leathers looks incongruous in an airport; it captures his attention. But who can it be? As soon as he sees the figure leave, Griffiths springs into action and scrambles down the staircase towards the Lufthansa check-in desk.

*

Griffiths approaches Elisabeth and asks her bluntly: "Who was the last person you called?".

"Wagner. Why?"

Griffiths quickly glances at his watch: "No, just before that."

She looks perplexed: "Andrew, but I got no response."

Without another word, Griffiths turns, runs.

*

In the car park Jax starts the bike up, puts on her crash helmet and leaves cautiously, trying to get used to handling the Yamaha on the slippery surface. She doesn't register that behind her – just a short distance - Griffiths has almost caught up with her on foot. He looks around to locate his car – frantically flicking the remote to find it - and finally gets into a white BMW. He starts the engine and pursues the Yamaha which is now almost out of sight.

*

Jax heads for the N201. In one of the mirrors, she suddenly notices a white BMW speeding behind her. Inside her crash helmet her eyes are darting from the road to the speedo, to the mirror and back. Shit! He's driving too fast; changing lanes and now too damn close behind her. She risks another glance in the mirror. It doesn't look like a police car; unless it's unmarked. But why pursue her? She's not speeding. Unless it's someone else. But who? She's been meticulous in her planning so far: the disguise, the ferry, the Tulip, Die Port van Cleve and Hôtel de L'Europe. Nobody in the world knows what she's been up to. Not even Lucia. Not yet.

She's frightened, the old pang of fear. Her heart is pounding, mouth dry. She's being threatened, she's sure. An exit is coming up and she's in the outside lane. The mirror. The BMW is right behind her, tailgating. At the last possible moment, she dangerously crosses lanes and swerves off the road, to a blare of angry car horns. The BMW is trapped in the outside lane and instantly overshoots the exit. At the top of the slip road, she brings the bike to a sharp stop, pulls off the helmet and screams.

Enemy

Motorway Services, A2 South Car Park, Holland

JAX PARKS UP THE motorbike and is fiddling with one of the panniers. She is wearing her crash helmet with the visor pulled down. Across in one of the car parking bays Griffiths pulls up in the BMW. He gets out and with a pair of binoculars observes her briefly. He locks the door and walks quickly across to her. Jax finally locks the pannier, aware of the presence of a man behind her. He clears his throat, to attract her attention, taps her on the back. The gesture is unwelcome.

"I wonder if I might have a word, please?" Griffiths tries his best to sound charming.

Jax stands upright, turns around and removes the crash helmet to reveal shoulder-length frizzy red hair, tinted glasses, heavy lipstick: "Usted habla Español?" ... do you speak Spanish?

He produces his ID and studies her face for a reaction: "No, I don't speak Spanish ... I'm looking for Andrew Flower."

She is more than confused, of course: "Si?"

And she immediately turns to walk away, towards the restaurant area, but he takes her elbow. She looks at him, then at his hand and brushes it off contemptuously.

Griffiths tries again: "My name is Mr Griffiths, HMRC Inspector." He thrusts the ID at her again, not used to such rejection.

Jax persists in very broken English: "You are police – inspector? No?"

"Not exactly, no ... probably more important." The joke inevitably falls flat.

"Soy Eva Flores, una famosa bailarina Española." I am Eva Flores, a famous Spanish dancer.

"You were at Schiphol airport, earlier. I saw you there."

Jax's Spanish accent is heavy and convincing: "Aeroporto? No."

He persists rudely. "Sure?"

"You police? Yes? No? Pregunta simple."

Griffiths makes to pursue her one more time but thinks better of it. Just as she turns to the restaurant, he takes photographs of the bike and her with his iPhone. He smiles smugly to himself: Clever me, always ahead.

*

In the ladies' rest room, Jax leans over the washbasin and looks in the mirror: she sees apprehension in her eyes. But she also sees and feels resilience: Andrew has cheated her. She must survive. The plan must work. She unzips her leathers and takes out her ferry ticket. Calais to Dover. One way, foot passenger.

'I wonder how long it will take me to get there?' she says to herself and gathers her belongings for the next part of her journey. But did Griffiths buy her story that she was Eva, a famous Spanish dancer?

South

A2 Motorway South, Holland

JAX RIDES THE MOTORBIKE SOUTH. She is checking her mirrors, watching other vehicles. Neither Griffiths nor the white BMW was there when she came out of the ladies' rest room ... so where is it now?

Another glance in the mirror. Damn! The BMW is there again. She glances at her speedo: 120 km/hr. She accelerates, head down, weaving in and out of the traffic. Horns blare, cars swerve. It's touch and go if she'll make it. The BMW is still there in the outside lane, so he just can't change lanes to catch her.

The speedo again – 140 km/hr. The engine is revving hard as she powers ahead. The BMW is catching up. But it's busy: cars, trucks, coaches. Then she pulls over to the right hand, inside lane and slows down to the speed of the other vehicles. The BMW is trapped in the line of fast-moving traffic in the outside lane. Once again, he can't get across to catch her.

She flips the visor up and breathes a sigh of relief. Her speedo is now down to 60km/hr. Ahead is an exit. She leaves the

A2 and rides up the slip road, her confidence restored.

*

Inside the BMW, Griffiths is fuming. He smashes the steering wheel with his fist in anger. Now he must risk a call to Elisabeth to update her. He takes the phone out of his pocket but drops it down into the footwell. Restrained by the seat belt, he can't lean down to retrieve it. He screams so loud that it burns his throat. He looks up in time to see the back of a Dutch HGV and jams on the brake – but his phone is trapped under the pedal – he's going to collide into it and there's nothing he can do.

Calais

Port of Calais Ferry Terminal, France

JAX WALKS FROM A QUIET CORNER of the car park towards the ferry terminal. She has abandoned the Yamaha and removed the Dutch number plate from de Groot. She's left the keys in the ignition. It's asking to be stolen and it probably won't take long.

Inside the terminal, she makes her way over to check-in to travel back as a foot passenger. But she can't help thinking about Griffiths: he can't possibly know who she is, she's been too careful. But what she had witnessed at Schiphol still mystifies her: Who is Elisabeth Deluc if not Andrew's lover? And what is the connection between her, Griffiths, and the other man?

*

At the foot passenger check-in, Jax produces her American passport and the one-way ticket to Dover. Jacqueline Donovitch from North Carolina is checked in without question by a bored French attendant. Her attire is now normal, she's discarded her leathers in favour of a dress and jacket. All she carries is the stuff sack containing the remaining contents of Andrew's attaché case.

Once in London, Jax leaves Victoria Station, complete with her stuff sack, and walks quickly towards the taxi rank.

The Dorchester Hotel

Park Lane, London, England

IN THE BACK OF A BLACK CAB, Jax finally breathes a sigh of relief. She looks out at Hyde Park, lost in thought, reliving the last twenty-four hours. On arrival at the hotel, her iPhone buzzes. She pays the driver and gets out to take the call. She looks at the screen: Christopher Fielding.

She tries to sound casual and uses his nickname: "Chase, hi! What's up?"

Fielding's tone is serious: "Hello Jax. Do you know where Andrew is?"

"Holland, as far as I know. Something I can help you with?"

A sigh of frustration: "He's not answering his mobile. People – ah – people are trying to reach him."

She walks towards the hotel's entrance and lowers her voice: "You sound weird, Chase. What people? People at the plant, you mean? Is something wrong? Is Mick alright?"

Fielding hesitates: "Oh. Oh, it's nothing really. I'll try him again later. No matter. Thanks." He hangs up and she heads into reception.

*

In the hotel lobby area, she meets Lucia Paluzzi. She looks glamorous: Versace and Gucci haute couture. They hug daintily, so as not to spoil Lucia's meticulously applied make-up.

Lucia looks at her friend: "I got your text from the ferry terminal. How did it all go?"

Jax laughs: "Let's go up to the Rooftop Bar for a drink and I'll explain everything."

"Okay, be mysterious. I've already checked us both in and looked at our suite. Luxurious is not the word, darling. It's positively regal!"

Jax squeezes her shoulder affectionately and they walk to the lift. Once inside, Jax says: "You wouldn't believe how mysterious, Lu. Really. I need a shower and I deserve that drink. I think we should have dinner at the Dorchester Grill tonight. My treat."

Lucia is impatient: "Yes, of course. But it went ok, Jax? Whatever you did over there in Amsterdam. Just tell me. I've been worried."

Police Station

Bethel Street Police Station, Norwich, Norfolk

LUCIA IS DRIVING A CLASSIC VW Karmann Ghia. It pulls up outside the police station. Jax opens the door: “Wish me luck.”

“You don’t need luck, Jax. All you need is you.”.

*

Once inside the station Jax is greeted at the counter by Sergeant Andy McPherson. She explains that her husband has gone missing in Holland, and she’s not heard from him. She’s terribly worried he might have had an accident, or worse. She just needs help.

“Right, Mrs Flower, I think you should speak to DI Quince. He has a good contact in the Amsterdam central police. Lucky, we’re quiet. One moment, please.”

McPherson – Mac to his friends and colleagues - picks up the phone. His smile to Jax says: yes. And he continues: “You’re lucky to get a DI. Fill in this form. Name, address, DOB. All the normal. Same for your husband. DI Quince will see you after. Is that okay?"

"Sure. Thanks." Jax takes the form and starts filling it in.

Interview

Bethel Street Police station, Norwich

MAC ESCORTS JAX to a well-organised open-plan office. Behind a desk sits Detective Inspector Peter Quince. He's a former front-row forward from County Dublin; late thirties, ex-Merchant Navy and full of old-world charm. Quince stands as Mac introduces them and hands Quince the form. He beckons her to sit and starts to read, occasionally looking up at Jax as he does so.

After a few moments he says: "Alright, now. I'm getting a picture. When exactly did your husband disappear?" His manner is engaging and sympathetic.

"He went over to Holland this Monday 13th June. Stena Line from Harwich 2300hrs crossing."

"And you've not heard from him since?"

"No."

"Today's Wednesday, is it not? 15th? That's only a few days. Two to be precise."

"Oh, he often goes over to Amsterdam or somewhere for a few days ... except ..."

Quince leans back in his chair: "Except what, Mrs Flower?"

"He always calls, just to check in. Even if only for a minute or so."

"And?"

"This time he didn't and he's not answering his mobile either. And he always does. So, I called his hotel direct. The Dam Square Inn."

"And?"

"The manager told me they haven't seen him since he checked in. His luggage is still in the room, packed. They don't think the bed was slept in on Tuesday night; reception checked with the chamber maid."

"Alright, yes."

"He normally stays at the Inn three days or so ... that's his routine."

"I see. Did he have a car?"

She nods: "Yes, but I don't know where it is. A parking garage somewhere in Amsterdam, I guess. I don't know if the Inn has a car park." She sounds fraught.

"Right." Quince pauses a moment. "Got any friends over there, has he?"

The way he says friends makes her think twice. What does he mean? Jax shoots Quince a suspicious glance: "What sort of friends?"

"Any sort, Mrs Flower."

"No, no I don't think so. I don't know." She frowns; a

moment of tension.

Quince resumes, matter-of-fact: “I see. When’s he due back? He had a return ferry ticket, I would presume. That would be normal?”

Jax shakes her head. Her expression says – how would I know? But she doesn’t articulate it. Quince is no fool and he is watching her, his years of experience evaluating her story so far. He leans forward, continues:

“Mrs Flower, just how worried about him are you?”

She stumbles: “What-what- do you mean?”

He smiles warmly to show her he’s sympathetic: “I mean, there are several possible explanations. The obvious one is an accident and that’s easily checkable with a single phone call to the Dutch authorities.”

Her voice sounds hollow: “If I don’t hear from him by tonight, I will be seriously worried.”

“Ok. Where’s he based? His work I mean.”

“The Flower Group, right here in Norwich.”

“Ah, yes. Pet foods and suchlike. That Flower?”

Jax nods.

“And have they not heard from your husband either?”

Jax thinks about Christopher Fielding: “No.”

“Do you want me to file a formal Missing Person Report, Mrs Flower?”

She hesitates: “I don’t know.” She thinks to herself: What’s the normal procedure? What do I do?

Quince can see her confusion and understands her predicament: “Tell you what now. Why don’t we just wait until tomorrow? If your instinct tells you he might call you tonight ..."

She manages a brave smile: "Yes, I think so. That would make sense."

For the first time he can see what a beautiful woman she is, but why is he thinking of a black widow?

"Meanwhile, I'll speak to my Superintendent and see what he thinks. But I must advise you. If your husband disappeared outside of the UK, then it will be largely out of our jurisdiction."

"I see."

"More a matter for the Dutch police and of course the Embassy. Or even Interpol."

Jax looks forlorn, so Quince makes a decision. But it is not just made out of understanding the difficulty of her predicament; he genuinely wants to help her.

"Give me the make and registration number of the car. At least I can get the ball rolling. If I don't hear from you before, might I call in on you at home tomorrow afternoon? Your full address is here on this form?"

"Yes, but may I have a piece of paper?"

Quince tears a piece of post-it note off a pad and hands it to her. She sketches a rough map for him and says out loud at the same time:

"Brook House is quite remote. It's well off the Norwich Road and your Satnav may take you to the house next door. It's happened before ...there you are ... it's down a long driveway off the main road."

"Thank you. So, tomorrow, Mrs Flower? Late afternoon if I don't hear from you first. About 4.30. All your husband's contact details are on the form? Mobile phone number, email address."

"It's all there, plus the company numbers."

Quince watches her as she leaves the interview room. What an extraordinary lady, he thinks to himself. Because there is something about her he just can't define or describe: an enigmatic quality.

*

In Quince's office sometime later, twenty-five-year-old WPC Helen Ross is taking instructions from him. She's blonde, vibrant and very thorough.

Quince says: "Oh, yes. And while you're at it, get on to Stena Line in Harwich, will you? I want details of the Monday evening sailing to Holland. Audi Q4 Sportback, registration number AWF 444.The passenger's name is Andrew Flower. OK, Rossi?"

"Yes, Guv." She writes quickly in her Police notebook; the kind of officer who likes to do things properly. And by the book. "Anything else?"

"Yes, actually. See if you can find out if there was anyone else travelling with him and the return date on the ticket. I'll contact my mate Cas in Amsterdam."

"Something suspicious, Guv?"

"Belt and braces, Rossi," he says in his sing-song manner. "You know my little ways."

She smiles because she does.

Forum

Millennium Plain, Norwich

OUTSIDE THE POLICE STATION, Jax gets into Lucia's VW and shuts the door with a distinctive and characteristic clunk.

She turns to her friend: "You know what I can't understand, Lu?"

Lucia pulls away, careful with the temperamental old gearbox; her eyes are fixed on the road: "Who was the other man with Elisabeth at Schiphol?"

Jax agrees: "Yeah, who? And what did she say? 'Let's get back to base'. What's that all about?"

"Andrew believed he was running off with her. But what if he wasn't?"

Jax sighs: "Yeah. And this creep Griffiths? Why were they all at Schiphol together? What do they know, huh? I don't get it."

Lucia stops at a red light: "Why do you think Griffiths chased after you?"

"I can only think he must have found a connection between Elisabeth and me. But what? And more importantly, how?"

"Who knows?" Lucia turns to Jax: "What was Quince like then, Jax?"

"Quite a hunk, southern Irish I would say." She pauses. "Anyway, he's stopping by the house tomorrow afternoon. As far as he's concerned, I spent Monday and Tuesday with you at the Dorchester. And Harrod's shopping."

"Si! And you bought a very expensive dress with your American Express card. I must say you were very extravagant, Mrs Flower."

"No, Lu. You were very extravagant. £675 for a Max Mara silk dress I'll probably never wear."

"At least it's your size," Lucia says and speeds away the second the lights change.

De Pablos

Flower Group, Conference Room, Norwich

CHRISTOPHER FIELDING SITS in the conference room with his iPhone and plays the message again. He looks worried. The message is from Señor De Pablos – Senior – in America.

"I am out of dialysis now, Mr Fielding. My son tells me he has trouble in speaking to Andrew. What is going on? Please get back to me. We need to progress, and we can't complete the company acquisition without Andrew, can we? And he certainly needs to speak to the agent about auctioning Brook House off ... to the highest bidder."

Clue

Quince's Office, Bethel Street Police Station, Norwich

THE PHONE RINGS AND QUINCE picks up, glancing at the caller display automatically.

0031 20 628 3966 (GEMEENTEPOLITIE AMSTERDAM)

"Quince! Cas Van Der Maas. How are you?"

Quince is pleased to hear from his friend: "Cas, good to hear from you! Still investigating counterfeit art and dodgy Rembrandts?"

"Not without your help, Quince! It isn't the same without a few pints of Guinness in Dam Square! So, you are investigating this Flower disappearance?"

"Yes. Although we haven't filed a misper, yet."

Cas understands the colloquial term for missing person: "Ok. But my office received your email about an Audi, English plates, missing in Amsterdam, which we have now found. But firstly, a background story connected to both the car and the driver."

Quince laughs out loud: "Oh, well I love a story. You know I do, Cas. Folk tales are in my blood. Recount your story so I can conjure up a mental image."

Quince listens avidly. But half of his attention is on Helen Ross, who is looking particularly charming today in civilian clothes.

Quince says: "Curious – why would our Mr Flower leave his credit card and so much cash on the table in the hotel restaurant? Doesn't make sense to me."

Cas agrees: "It's as if he wanted to be remembered."

Quince purses his lips: "There's no suggestion of an abduction or a kidnapping? No threats or ransom demands?"

"Nothing at all. My team has contacted all the regional casualty units. No sign of him. He seems to have walked out of the Die Port van Cleve restaurant and disappeared. He didn't return to the Tulip Hotel – where he told the waiter he was going - we checked with the receptionist, Anna Brun."

Helen watches Quince doodling a sketch: "What else was in the hotel room? Any personal belongings of any interest?"

"Just the usual items for travel: clothes, toiletries etc. He obviously intended to return."

Helen comes over and looks at what he is sketching.

"Yes. Or meant us to believe he would."

Cas agrees. "What shall we do with the car? There were no keys to the Audi at the Tulip."

"Can you tow it?"

"Yes, but not easily. I'd need men and a low loader ..." He pauses, suggesting you know how it is with time and police budget.

"Cas, leave it with me for 24 hours. I'll speak to Flower's wife and discuss it with Superintendent Brian Cragg and thanks for telling me your little Amsterdam story. Very interesting."

"Tot ziens, Quince." Cas says warmly: 'see you – so long.'

Quince looks at Helen: "Pop in and get Mac will you, Helen."

A moment later Sergeant Andy McPherson comes into Quince's office with a quizzical expression. He says 'Sir' in deference to Helen.

Quince looks up: "Ah, Mac. Find out all you can about the Flower Group. Local and National papers, business news. You know the routine."

"Information gathering?"

"Exactly. I need to get a clearer picture."

Mac scribbles down some notes on his pad and leaves. Helen comes over to Quince and looks at what he has been sketching. A woman's oval-shaped face, long dark hair. And a question mark.

Quince looks up at her: "Curious, don't you think, Helen?"

Complex

Brook House, Salhouse, Norfolk

THE SWIMMING POOL COMPLEX at the Flower's residence is stunning and tastefully in-keeping with the rest of the building. A shimmering blue pool with underwater lights, high Scandinavian-style pine ceiling; Italian mosaic floor tiles. A bar area with sun loungers and tables.

In the pool Jax is swimming through the illuminated water: front crawl and backstroke. She gets out of the pool, removes her goggles and puts on a towelling bathrobe, drying her hair with a small towel. She wanders through the house, simultaneously drying her hair. The front doorbell chimes.

She opens the front door and stands there in her bathrobe. Her hair is now wrapped up in a towel like a turban, the way she does. Outside, Quince admires the gleaming TR4A, still shiny with rainwater.

"You're very prompt, Mr Quince. Please come in."

Quince hesitates, surprised by her casual appearance: "I have news from the Dutch police, Mrs Flower."

Her hand shoots up to her mouth in shock: "What ..."

"They've ..."

She gasps: "They've found him?" She leans against the door, a credible piece of acting. "No."

Quince puts his hand on her forearm, just a touch: "Only his car, I'm afraid, Mrs Flower, only his car ... is now convenient?"

"Sure, yes." She opens the front door wider and gestures him in. Behind Quince are several uniformed officers.

Quince feels awkward: "Thank you. I'll not keep you long. My colleagues will search the gardens if you don't mind. There is always the possibility of an accident ...or something possibly overlooked. I hope that's alright with you. Standard procedure. I can obtain a warrant if you wish?"

"No, that's fine. Do what you must." They walk into the hallway, and she gestures him to follow her. "Come on through, Detective Inspector Quince."

"Quince is fine." He follows her into a modern conservatory, luxuriously appointed: "What's that I can smell? Chlorine?"

"Oh yes. The pool. A lot of maintenance but we think it's worth it."

Along one side is a huge window, through which the swimming pool complex can now be clearly seen. They sit on soft garden chairs.

She eyes him and wets her lips: "So?" She pauses: "I thought we hadn't decided on a course of action just yet. When we were in your office, we said we'd wait twenty-four hours. Wasn't that your suggestion, Quince?" A slight frown.

"Yes, but ..."

"So why are you investigating Andrew's disappearance when I haven't officially reported him as missing?" She smiles to show him she is not complaining, just politely asking, the frown has now vanished.

"I said, Mrs Flower, if you recall, that I would get the ball rolling. You gave me the car's registration number."

"I did, yes. You are right. Sorry. I wasn't trying to make a point. Far from it." The conflict she's creating, putting Quince on the defensive is exactly what she had intended all along. And he's played into her hand, unwittingly.

Quince takes a breath: "The Dutch police discovered his car in an underground car park and the hotel where he was staying. It all happened because a restaurant manager reported your husband's gold credit card and two fifty-euro notes were left at a table ... accidentally, one assumes."

She waits a moment: "This is all very quick."

"Mrs Flower, is there any way your husband could have planned to ...? I don't know ..."

Jax stands and walks over to the conservatory window and fiddles with a large rubber plant. Her back is now to Quince.

He continues: "... vanish for some reason? I assume you have a happy – life – there is no chance he was – running away? Or in any danger. These are questions I must ask you."

She turns round, her face a blank. She wanders back to him, rubs her eye with the cuff of her gown: "No. We're happy. As you can see, we have everything." She sits back down as he continues:

"The Dutch police have had no reports of any accidents,

attacks, suicides or murders of any unidentified foreigners. We must assume that he vanished voluntarily."

Jax nods vacantly. Quince is very taken with Jax. And she knows it: "Voluntarily? Such an odd way of putting it? Can you vanish involuntarily?"

"Yes. You can be abducted – kidnapped – and held for a ransom. But by now you'd have received a demand, wouldn't you?"

"Yes."

"And you haven't?"

"No, Quince. I haven't."

"Then assuming he's alive and well, he could be almost anywhere." He pauses a moment. "Actually, my Superintendent has asked me to go to Holland on another matter. I could, if you like, collect the Audi on your behalf ..." He's dangling the bait for her. "Unless, of course, you are happy to go over there and ... collect it yourself?"

She looks him in the eye; this is going much better than she could have possibly dreamed: "No, no. That's very kind ... if you are going there anyway ... it would make perfect sense. Thank you for suggesting it, Quince. I'm very appreciative."

"Not at all, Mrs Flower. It's a pleasure. I'll need the keys. Assuming you have a spare set here in the house."

She smiles at a memory: Plop. The key fob sinking into the river Amstel. "Follow me." She stands. Quince does the same: "You're from the States?"

"Yeah. Two of them really: Charlotte, North Carolina. Then New York."

He wanders past an antique table and looks at a silver-framed wedding photo. It is engraved: 'Churchman House Registry Office, Norwich.' The bride and groom and another very stylishly-attired couple.

"Lovely picture," Quince says with a smile. "I know exactly where that is."

Jax sighs and picks it up: "Yeah, our wedding day and it didn't rain." She stares at the photo reflectively. "So, this lady here is my best friend Lucia, my maid of honour. That's Christopher Fielding, Andrew's business partner and best man. The stunning couple in the middle are Andrew and I." She laughs to show she is joking. "Five years ago, last Friday, as a matter of fact."

Quince shares the joke: "A very stunning couple indeed, Mrs Flower. Your friend – and best man - Mr Fielding looks familiar for some reason."

"Oh, Chase was always in the local newspapers a few years back. He was on so many committees: Rotary, Masonic, you name it. He was also on the Board of Directors at the Norfolk and Norwich University Hospital. Always photographed somewhere."

"That must be it then, a newspaper."

"And he was a lawyer, before he worked for Andrew – so you might have seen him in court," Jax grins at Quince. "Always on the side of the good guy." She replaces the photo onto the table, being careful not to scratch the highly-polished wood. And adjusts it so it sits in line with the others.

He smiles: "How did you meet your husband, if you don't

mind my asking?"

"London. An auction at Sotheby's." She doesn't want to talk about Andrew, so she moves on swiftly. "Will you return his belongings from the hotel to me personally, Quince? And the Audi, of course."

"I will. Oh, and by the way, whilst I'm here ..."

She looks mildly alarmed: "Yes."

"Can you tell me your whereabouts while your husband was away in Amsterdam? Last Monday and Tuesday? That will be the 13th and 14th June?"

She bites her lips and pauses: "Yes, of course. I was in London with Lucia. To help kill some time while Andrew was away."

"I see. I'm sorry I have to ask."

"That's ok, sure. We stayed at the Dorchester. We often go to London to shop for clothes in Harrod's. Maybe take in a show. It was Lucia who found me the car on the drive; a surprise anniversary gift for Andrew."

The mention of the car and its significance is awkward, he says simply: "Ah, the TR4A, lovely."

Jax nods a 'yes' and he follows her out towards the hallway: "He keeps the spare keys for all his cars in the study. Andrew has quite a collection. Come this way ..."

*

Quince follows her into the study and sees assorted car memorabilia. Jax unlocks the door of a key safe mounted on the wall. Inside there are a number of other keys and fobs with logos: Jaguar – Aston Martin – Ferrari – Bentley. He sees a die-cast model of a Mercedes Benz 300SLR racing car on the desk. The number 722 is painted on the side.

"The famous 722. The Holy Grail!" says Quince with enthusiasm.

"Stirling Moss is his ultimate hero, yes. As you probably know, he won the Mille Miglia in 1955."

"I think every schoolboy of my vintage knows that. It seems your husband and I have something in common. That's good."

"Yes, isn't it?" Jax pauses. "This looks like the spare Audi key fob. Here you are." Jax hands the fob to him and he follows her to the front door.

"Thank you, Mrs Flower. I'll be in touch."

"So long, Quince. And please thank your boss from me."

The uniformed officers are on the driveway. One of them shakes his head to indicate they have found nothing in the grounds of Brook House. Quince nods his understanding.

Observer

Norwich Road, Salhouse, Norfolk

AT THE BOTTOM OF HER DRIVE, across the road, is a grey Peugeot 2008 GT. On the back window is an Enterprise Rent-A-Car Amsterdam sticker. Behind the wheel of the left-hand drive car sits Elisabeth Deluc. The driver's side window is open and she is taking photos with her mobile phone. Neither Jax nor Quince can see her, because from this vantage point the sweep of the drive obscures her from view.

On her lap is a notebook with a list of addresses, with house details from various Norfolk estate agents. To the casual observer – and if asked – she is looking for property on behalf of a wealthy Dutch client. She watches the uniformed police officers pile into an unmarked vehicle and make its way down the drive. She makes a note of the time and waits.

Next, she sees a well-built man follow the police vehicle in a battered Renault. Could this be the investigating officer? If so, what exactly is he investigating?

She makes another note – including the Renault's

registration number – and ends with a blunt, solid question mark: why are the police there?

Mac

Bethel Street Police Station, Norwich

QUINCE WALKS into the open-plan main office; there is an air of excitement. Mac and WPC Helen Ross are hunched over a computer with a stack of papers and photocopies spread out on the desk.

Mac's enthusiasm is boundless: "Guv! Guv! Guv! A result!"

Quince is his normal, stoic self: "What is it, Mac? I'm on a mission."

"Just come and have a quick look."

Helen joins in: "This first; East Anglian Daily Times. Four years ago. Have a read." She hands him a photocopy of the front page of the paper and he reads it out loud to Mac and Helen:

"Local businessman killed in puzzle car accident ... Company Director, Nigel Flower, was killed in a car accident on the Norwich Ring Road near Grapes Hill. Police are investigating. The likely cause was a split in the brake line causing the hydraulic fluid to leak out. Investigators believe the split may have been caused by normal wear and tear. Widow Isabelle is devastated. Interesting, but is this relevant?"

Mac is still excited: "Now look at this, two months ago. FX Trading Statement." He hands Quince another photocopied document.

Quince takes it and resumes reading: "It was announced today that the Flower Group is to be bought by the De Pablos Corporation - a South American chemical giant - for an undisclosed sum. Alright, so what?"

Mac looks at Helen to garner support: "I spoke to a journalist on the Financial Times. Flower Group are about to conclude a deal. The figure is rumoured to be around the hundred-million-pound mark. Very hush-hush."

Quince brightens: "That's an awful lot of pet food, is it not, Mac?"

"You think about it, Guv; the main plant is huge. The company owns acres of land too. And my contact said the company is very profitable."

Quince says: "And the owner of it all has gone missing in Holland. Well, well, Mac. Yes, this is a tantalising angle on the story so far. Helen?"

"And his brother died in a mysterious car accident. I'll follow it up shall I, Guv?" Helen looks at Quince.

Mac: "So, what are we talking about here? Murder? Suicide? What?"

The three of them are silent until Helen says: "Or Jacqueline killed him. She has motive. Acres of it."

"But why? She doesn't need money. She's loaded. And where's the body? Yes, follow this up, Rossi. Well done, both of you. Good job." But there is something in his tone of voice which says he doesn't mean it. Helen and Mac make a face at each other as Quince turns away. And then he looks back as if to say 'what?'

"I wonder if Andrew Flower has a will?" Helen asks.

Quince turns back: "Why? Because he's wealthy?"

"Yes," says Helen with a twinkle. "And she stands to inherit the lot. They have no children to consider."

"The poor bugger's not even dead yet, is he?" Quince raises his eyebrows, turns again and starts to leave. "At least, we haven't found him yet."

Password

Andrew's Office, Flower Group, Norfolk

THE DEAD OF NIGHT and Lucia's Karmann Ghia glides along the Ring Road. She is gradually getting used to the Judson supercharged engine. And, although only a 1.19cc, the left-hand drive coupé sounds throaty. She executes a nifty gear change as they pull up just down the road from the plant, out of sight. Lucia turns to Jax with a look of amusement.

"Steady on, Lu, this isn't the Italian Job," Jax says with a laugh.

"Says who, bella? On days like these!" She hums the tune and Jax laughs again, loudly.

"Ha!"

*

Outside the main entrance of the building, Jax takes the master key card from Andrew's wallet and pushes it into the slot of the door entry security system. It clicks, the lock releases and the door opens automatically.

She looks over her shoulder and goes in. Once inside she sees the familiar wall-mounted digital control box. She taps the six-digit code onto the keypad; the alarm and CCTV are immediately disarmed. The plant is deserted, just the sound of the generators and the air conditioning buzzing. She runs through to the narrow steel staircase up to the gantry, hardly catching her breath. She makes her way towards the admin offices, not glancing over the rail. She runs through admin as far as Andrew's office.

Jax sits at the desk, turns Andrew's computer on and punches in the vital combination of letters and numbers that form the password: 1000-MIGLIA-722-MOSS. The computer accepts the code, and she clicks to email. She scrolls through Andrew's inbox quickly until she sees:

JUAN DE PABLOS, PRESIDENT OF DE PABLOS CORPORATION, TO ANDREW FLOWER AND CHRISTOPHER FIELDING.

'Please accept this statement as an Agreement in principle for De Pablos Corporation (USA) to purchase the Flower Group (Norwich) Ltd for £100 million. Our lawyers will draw up contracts. Deposit of £10 Million will be paid into the Flower/Fielding account at: ABN AMRO BANK. Gustav Mahlerlaan 10, Amsterdam, Holland, as requested. The balance to be paid on exchange of contracts in Miami. Funds to be transferred by us to your account Banque Privée, Rothschild, Cayman Islands. Acquisition to include processing plants, land, all assets commercial and residential, as agreed.'

Although much of this she knew from the two documents in the soft-leather folder she had discovered in the attaché case, the private bank in the Caymans was something new. More betrayal. She prints out three pages, quietly watching them drop into the tray. Her mind is wild: this is even worse than she had thought in the hotel suite back in Amsterdam.

She runs out of the building, reactivating all the alarms she had turned off when she entered and jumps into Lucia's waiting VW.

*

Lucia's brown eyes shine in the reflection from the dashboard: "Anything, Jax?"

Jax clenches the three pages of printout: "Everything, Lu. Everything. What did he think I was going to do? Go on the street and beg?"

Lucia starts the engine: "I doubt you even crossed his mind. Andrew's not the type for second thoughts, is he?"

Griffiths

Andrew Flower's Office, Flower Group, Norwich

FIELDING HAD BEEN ABOUT to go for a jog when Griffiths had turned up unexpectedly. Fielding is wearing a black Valentino designer track-suit and a look of impatience at the intrusion. His schedule meant nothing to Griffiths.

They are sitting either side of a cluttered desk. The interview has now been in progress for some time. They are certainly not the most likely combination for a lasting friendship: Griffiths, the apparently covetous taxman; Fielding, the consummate executive and bon viveur.

Griffiths says: "And I'll need copies of the Flower Group company accounts for the last six financial years. Certified by a legitimate chartered accountant." He emphasises the last three words as if to make a point.

"Our accounts are filed by Fry, Dodd and Artisan. They are most certainly legitimate, Mr Griffiths." Fielding's fingers sweep through his coiffed silver-grey hair, his eyes shine with anger.

Griffiths ignores the rebuff.

Suddenly Fielding's iPhone buzzes and he takes it out of his track-suit pocket. He looks at the screen: JUAN DE PABLOS SNR and a long number.

"Feel free to answer it, Mr Fielding."

"Just my ex-wife's mother ..."

"Your former mother-in-law, then?" Griffiths corrects him unnecessarily.

"Yes."

"The famous Delta McQueen QC, is it?" Griffiths says knowingly.

Fielding is surprised: "Yes. How do you know?"

"A competent detective gathers information, Mr Fielding," Griffiths looks self-satisfied. "You and Nina Fielding were never shy of the media, were you? Charity events and so forth. Neither is Mrs McQueen, with respect."

Fielding tries to conceal his anger: "I thought police were the detectives here in Norwich, Mr Griffiths. You're a tax inspector. At least, you are according to your business card."

Griffiths smiles, water off a duck's back: "I'm a forensic accountant, Mr Fielding. Which brings me to another question."

Fielding turns his phone off: "Yes."

"Where is Andrew Flower?" Griffiths asks bluntly.

"Holland ... yes, Amsterdam."

"Have you spoken to him today?"

Fielding replies: "No, I haven't. Not yet, that is."

Griffiths moves on: "I'll also need details of any cash transfers to or from overseas accounts. You know the situation.

The Revenue are sharp on money laundering and so forth."

"Money laundering? Andrew would have to ..."

But Griffiths cuts him off: "Cooperate. And so will you, Mr Fielding."

Fielding stares at the papers on the desk.

Griffiths' tone is patronising: "Forty-eight hours should be enough. I'll see myself out. Have an excellent day, won't you, Mr Fielding." Griffiths stands and starts to walk out of Andrew's office. "Oh, by the by, Fry, Dodd and Artisan?"

"Yes."

"Very competent firm of accountants. They'll do their best for you, of that, I am sure. Good day."

Fielding feels unsettled: how does Griffiths know so much about him?

Very Irrésistible

Brook House, Salhouse, Norfolk

SEVEN IN THE MORNING and Jax sits behind the desk in Andrew's study. Rachmaninov plays quietly in the background. She is scrutinising the three sheets of printout. Suddenly the front doorbell chimes. She's not expecting anyone this early in the morning and did not hear a car on the drive.

She walks through the hallway to the front door and looks through the spy hole. Through the fisheye lens she sees the image of Hywel Griffiths proffering his ID card. She immediately recognises him and is shocked. She steps back and instinctively pulls her towelling bathrobe more tightly around her. She opens the front door slowly and cautiously. He steps forward and stares at her.

"What the hell time you call this, whoever you are?"

"I'm looking for Mr Flower. Andrew Flower."

The ID is still held out for her inspection. She yawns, glances at it: "He's not here. What do you want?"

"A quiet word. You are Mrs Flower?"

She nods sleepily: “Yeah. About what?”

“Your husband, mainly. It is important.”

“It’s seven in the morning. I’m barely dressed. Can’t it wait?”

“I’m afraid not ... may I?” He edges forward respectfully. “Please?”

Jax looks at the card more closely: “HMRC? I’m afraid I know nothing of his work. Do you have authority to be here?”

He smiles, attempting charm: “Yes, of course I do. It really won’t take a moment ... since I’m here. I’d be most grateful to you.”

Jax is confused: “How did you get here? I didn’t hear a car pull up on the drive.” She looks out onto the driveway; it’s empty apart from the TR4A.

“Oh, I parked up on the main road and walked up the drive.”

Griffiths is now full of bonhomie; he needs to ingratiate himself to get her on-side. She admits him into the hallway. He looks around, not missing a detail.

“Are you quite sure he’s not here?”

“Quite sure, yeah.”

Griffiths regards her slowly and deliberately and then sniffs audibly: “Very Irrésistible?”

Jax is astounded, but gets it at once: “What?” She freezes inside, tries to compose herself.

Griffiths looks pleased he has touched a nerve: “Your fragrance ... Givenchy ... I’d recognise it anywhere. One of the girls in Signals used it ... on a night out on the town.”

“D-Did she?” She tries to summon a smile to cover up her utter shock at this comment. The moment is loaded with tension and suggestion: that, after all, vanity could be her undoing. She continues. "Oh ... yes ... very popular ... as well." She stares at him, trying to read his mind. She can't.

"Mrs Flower?"

"Yeah ... yes?"

"You went quiet ... I digress, I'm sorry. Then, where is he?"

"What?

Griffiths sighs, a hint of impatience: "Your husband. Where is he?"

"You tell me ..."

He knows he's unnerved her: "But I'm asking you, Mrs Flower."

"He, he left for Holland on Monday. I haven't heard from him since."

"You've contacted the Police?"

She nods, turns, walks towards the open kitchen door and he follows her. Suddenly he slips into the study, taking in every detail.

"I see animal slaughter pays well."

Jax zips past him. He sees the three pages of printout lying on the desk where she'd been reading them. She scoots around him quickly and picks them up: "Do you mind, these are private!" But she drops one. He quickly picks the page up, not taking his eyes off her. He's making a point because he knows he's deliberately invading her privacy.

"Oh, terribly sorry, Mrs Flower. Thought I was following you. No offence." He hands the page back to her. She puts it with the other two pages and lays them face down on top of all the other private documents.

Griffiths watches her carefully and continues: "I'll come straight to the point. HMRC are investigating your husband's company and his activities within it."

Jax says awkwardly: "I know nothing of this. You'll have to speak to the accountants, or to Christopher Fielding, Andrew's business partner. You see I'm really not the ..."

But Griffiths cuts her off sharply, maintaining a level voice: "Ah yes, Fielding. But the person I really need to speak to is ... Andrew ... isn't it?"

She flinches at the use of his first name, and he smiles. It always works; another raw nerve caressed.

Jax says: "Yes, but I've already told you. I am very, very worried about him."

"Of course, you would be."

Griffiths turns, walks into the hallway towards the front door. Then, his hand is on the door handle. He touches the fisheye lens with a knowing look: "I won't forget your cooperation at this early hour, Mrs Flower."

He looks at her for two seconds longer than is necessary: now he knows she saw him standing outside the front door ringing the doorbell. And he also knows the ploy of parking his car on the main road – to unnerve her – wasn't nearly as effective as it could have been.

Jax closes the front door after him and slumps back against it. She smells the fragrance on her wrists and forearm – Very Irrésistible – and sighs at her fundamental error of judgment.

But did he, could he possibly have made the connection with

the Spanish biker he encountered at the motorway services, Amsterdam. Eva Flores? Surely it was not possible. One thing was for absolute certain: from now on she'd have to watch it: Griffiths was as big an enemy as the rest of them put together.

Chase

The Flower Group, Norwich, Norfolk

JAX APPROACHES THE MAIN entrance of the plant and presses the intercom: "Christopher Fielding is expecting me." Jax looks at the CCTV.

"Good morning, Mrs Flower, please come in," says the receptionist.

*

Christopher Fielding sits at the conference table; he looks up, startled. He isn't expecting her, but he looks pleased to see her, nonetheless. Jax is calm, holding an A4 envelope, places it carefully onto the table and smiles:

"Hello, Chase. How's it goin'?" Jax is the only person permitted to call him 'Chase'. The name originally appeared in American comic books published by Marvel. She'd used it jokingly at first, but over the years, it had stuck. Christopher was too long-winded, she insisted; and he would never allow his name to be abbreviated to 'Chris' in a million years. It just isn't cricket, he'd said seriously. So, Chase it was.

He stands and kisses her decorously on both cheeks: "Wonderful, thank you, Jax. Lovely to see you. But the look on your exquisite punim says this visit isn't social?"

"No." She can't help but smile: the use of the Yiddish word for face amuses her.

"And you haven't got a bottle of Krug Grande Cuvée concealed in that envelope for me, have you?"

"No, I haven't."

"So, what's up? You'd better come and sit down, Jax. Tea? Coffee?"

"Nothing, thanks."

They sit at the table and Fielding looks at her expectantly: "Do tell."

"A delightful man called Hywel Griffiths came to see me this morning. I'd just got out of the shower."

"I see."

"Seven o'clock. Yeah. Griffiths wanted to know where Andrew is. So where is he?" She pauses for a few long moments. "The guy threatened me. Intimidation, I would say. He wanted answers, Chase."

Fielding looks awkward and can't hide it: "Holland? Amsterdam? I told you on the phone I can't get hold of him. No one can."

"Oh really. No one can." Jax waits. "Is that right?"

"Well, I can't, and neither can Jenny, the receptionist."

Jax takes a deep breath: "Let's cut the crap, Chase. You know what's going on."

"Ah, no ... I ..."

"How about running off to Miami with Elisabeth Deluc? Huh? How about that, for starters?"

Fielding's eyes are fixed on her. He can't believe what he is hearing as she continues, her tone is now flat: "And what about Juan De Pablos? Huh?"

"Jax, I ..."

"What about him, Chase? Some nifty little hundred-million-pound offshore tax deal. No wonder I get a personal visit from HMRC at the crack of dawn."

Fielding gulps: "I'm not sure I ...."

"I thought we were friends, Chase. Despite everything." Jax finds this very hard, because for many years they had been friends.

"We are, Jax. This is a ...."

"Humour me, Chase. Banque Privée Rothschild Caymans. Ring any bells with you? ABN AMRO HOLLAND?"

Fielding stands up slowly, tries to compose himself: "Okay, Jax, okay. He never caught the flight connection to Miami from Holland. I don't know why."

"Right. But you don't deny he was running off with her? An affair?"

"No, I don't. I can't."

"More than that, a bit of a game changer for all of us, right?"

"Yes, Jax. Yes."

"Look at me, Chase. Your complicity in the deal is obvious - you organised it. A hundred million pounds offshore. No tax and no wife to pay off. It's all here - in the agreement. No wonder

Griffiths is pissed off."

Jax produces the three sheets of printout from the envelope and puts them on the desk for him to see. He glances at them, shaking his head, completely caught out. She then picks them up and puts them back in the envelope: "Well?"

"It was Andrew's plan to exclude you from the deal. I don't know why. But you know what he's like. Unpredictable. I don't even know where he is as I've already told you."

"He's not very unpredictable when he plans so meticulously to cheat his wife ... and the authorities ... out of a fortune, right? Tax evasion is an imprisonable offence, isn't it, Chase?"

He shakes his head again: "Yes."

Jax looks him in the eye: "Listen to me, Chase. If you want a future, any future, you'd better help me. Or this goes to Griffiths and the police. I have nothing to lose, and I don't damn well care. Do you get it?"

Fielding is now trapped: "Yes, I get it, Jax. I don't know what to say."

She can't hide her rage: "Well, I do, Chase. I am sick of Andrew and his fucking affairs. Sick of the lies. His constant betrayal. Am I making myself clear?"

His voice is barely a whisper now: "Yes, you are. What do you want me to do, Jax?"

"Just wait for my call." She stands up.

"What about Andrew? Have you spoken to him?" There is something in his eyes, a flicker of something she can't read. And the tone of his voice ...

"I'd be more concerned about Griffiths if I were you. Really, I would. He's a dog with a bone and he ain't going away. You'd lose everything if he ever found out the truth about your dishonest business practice. And consequently ... so would I."

"I get it, Jax."

"Good. And yeah, we were friends, Chase. But I think that particular horse has bolted, don't you?"

She doesn't even wait for an answer. And, as the conference room door shuts behind her, Fielding takes out his phone and scrolls to 'contacts'.

*

Jax is about to leave the plant when she bumps straight into Mick, the factory foreman and chief slaughterman.

"Mrs Flower. Any news of your husband?"

"Why?"

"The police came to see me yesterday."

Jax is startled. "What did they want with you, Mick?"

"To tell me that you had reported Mr Flower as missing. And asked me when I'd last seen him."

"Oh? And what did you tell them?"

"It was one officer; a Sergeant McPherson, from Bethel Street nick."

"And?"

"I couldn't quite remember. Think it was that night you was here at the plant. Your anniversary. You said Mr Flower was buying you some roses from the Tesco Express, up the road, or something." He scratches his chin. He gives her a puzzling look, as if he knows more than he is saying.

"So I did, yes. You're right. I said he'd be chatting up the assistants, naughty me."

Mick moves closer to her: "But the thing is, I didn't see actually him, did I, Mrs Flower? And I'm not sure what to do. Sergeant McPherson wants me to make a formal statement."

Jax thinks about Quince: "Just tell the policeman the truth, Mick. If you didn't see him, you didn't see him, but thanks for telling me. You did the right thing. Must run."

Mick watches Jax walk away, slightly in awe: her beauty, the grace of her movement, the way she spoke to him with such understanding. Maybe he did see Andrew in the car park that night after all. He just couldn't remember. He'd had a long drive back from King's Lynn with a lorry full of carcasses and was tired. But if Mrs Flower – the beautiful American – says he was there, he was there.

He had Sgt McPherson's number; he'd call and book an appointment to make a statement.

Cragg

Bethel Street Police Station, Norwich

SUPERINTENDENT BRIAN CRAGG sits behind his desk; a world-weary police administrator with a depleted budget. He is holding Jacqueline Flower's statement. He's near retirement and the last thing he needs in his life are problems, complications, or unnecessary challenges. He has enough on his plate already. Quince is standing in front of the desk, looking anxious. It was he who gave Cragg the statement to read.

Cragg never lost his thick Birmingham accent: "You'd better have a damn good reason for investing all this time and energy, Quince. What is it?"

Quince eyes Cragg: "Andrew Flower is about to sell his company for an estimated £100 million pounds, and he's vanished off the face of the earth. He's either been kidnapped or murdered. His wife, Jacqueline, as you have now read, is very anxious to find out which."

"And which do you think it is? We're clearly missing two vital elements here – a ransom demand - or a body. Is there more?"

"Yes. Mac's been doing some digging. Mr Flower's brother Nigel died in a mysterious car accident a few years back. Mechanical failure was given as the cause."

Cragg is sceptical: "You think it was pre-meditated murder? Is that it? That these two, what, situations are connected?"

"It's surely more than coincidence?"

"Very well, Quince. If you believe Mrs Flower is in danger, I can't stop you from pursuing the case, but be wary of investing too much time and resource."

"I do believe she might be in danger, yes. And I'd like to discover more."

Cragg leans back in his chair and clasps his hands behind his head: "I take it that this coincidence involves you travelling over to Amsterdam?"

"Yes ... I can have a poke around ... try and gather some evidence, speak to some witnesses ... I could even try and retrieve Flower's car at the same time. Makes sense."

"You'll see your old mucker ... what was his name?"

"Cas van der Maas, central police Amsterdam. Yes, I will see him."

Cragg nods his head in comprehension and says quietly: "Amsterdam? A little off your beat to collect some woman's motor?"

Quince is ready for this because of what he has promised Jax and the untruth he told her: "I'm due some leave from Christmas. I could do it in my own time. And I don't mind dipping my hand in my pocket for the price of a dinky ferry ticket."

"Quite taken with her, are you, Quince? What's her name? Jacqueline Flower, an American lass?"

Quince purses his lips: "Yes, I am. But that has nothing to do with my concern for Mrs Flower's immediate welfare."

"Don't give me a load of old twaddle, matey – I'm too long in the tooth – so are you for that matter. Use two days of your leave to go there. But let me have your expenses and I'll reimburse you. My old boss in Edgbaston used to call it 'creative accounting.' Off you go and let me know what happens."

Quince: "I'll solve this, Superintendent."

"Oh, I have no doubt you will, DI Quince ... that's why I'm sanctioning your mission. I'll wheedle it out of my miserable budget somehow, don't you worry."

Cas

Elandsgracht, Amsterdam, Holland

AMSTERDAM'S POLICE HEADQUARTERS on Elandsgracht – Hoofdbureau Politie - is a sprawling collection of buildings beside the Singelgracht canal. In a conference room upstairs the Gemeentepolitie often discuss problems experienced by foreign nationals visiting the city: robberies, lost passports, misunderstandings in De Wallen – the red-light district; the list is endless. Today is no exception. The Dutch detectives have been told how much time they can allocate solving the mystery of a missing Englishman. And a recovered car.

Detective Cas van der Maas is a tall man, with a mop of unruly blond hair and a handsome face adorned by a walrus moustache. He is known all over the Netherlands as 'the King of Amsterdam' for his crusade against crime – roaring basso voice - and charismatic personality. He always wore a black leather jacket and Levi jeans, much to the annoyance of his superiors. The tee-shirts displaying American rock bands didn't add much to his sartorial elegance. But nobody seriously challenged him.

Today he is being admonished by one of those superiors – his boss – Inspector Joop van Durren, a neatly dressed man who looked more like a mortgage advisor than a policeman. They are standing outside Hoofdbureau, and Cas is looking at his watch.

They are speaking rapidly: "What I am saying, Cas," says van Durren, "is yes, by all means meet up with DI Quince, but don't spend too much of my dwindling budget on solving his English case. Is that clear?"

"Perfectly clear, sir," says Cas with a smile. But Quince is his friend and has helped him in the past when he needn't have.

"Ik hoop het." Van Durren hopes so but isn't convinced. In the end Cas is a law unto himself.

*

Quince walks from Central Station in the heart of Amsterdam towards Nieuwezijds Voorburgwal, a wide street. There are trams, cars, cyclists, and the perpetual movement of people.

Up ahead on the right he finds Gravenstraat and walks down to the the Dam Square Inn. He sees Cas standing outside talking on his iPhone. His discussion looks animated and intense, but as soon as he sees Quince, he hangs up. They shake hands and start to chat, immediately in tune with one another's lives and work. The small talk doesn't last long; they both have a job to do and are aware of police budgets on either side of the North Sea.

"So, Quince. This is the famous old Inn where Mr Flower checked in but didn't stay. His arrival is captured on street CCTV. The image is not too clear. But I have emailed it to you.

He certainly has better dress sense than me!"

Quince laughs and Cas continues: "We have collected his personal effects so they can relet the room. But my officer photographed every inch of it as Flower left it. His suitcase and suit carrier are in my car. I'll give them to you later."

"Ok."

"Let's go over to Hulscher's, the hotel's restaurant is an Amsterdam landmark.."

*

Quince and Cas cross over the road, walk into the restaurant and look around the lofty interior. Two men approach them. The older, puts out his hand and looks at Quince.

"Hello! Welcome! Detective Inspector Quince? I am Paul Van Wijk, the owner and this is Jasper, the waiter. Hello, Cas!" Cas and Van Wijk shake hands; speak in rapid Dutch.

Cas switches back to English: "So, Quince. Jasper is the waiter who served Mr Flower. His English is not so good, so Paul will explain."

Paul looks at Quince: "The only thing Jasper can remember, apart from the gold credit card and hundred euros in cash, is the wine. He ordered a Saracosa Governo Rosso 2020. It's a Tuscan red and we have just ordered a few cases to see how it goes. It's locals and tourists here and they drink mostly Dutch beer and Hollands."

"Hollands?" Quince is confused.

Cas explains: "Hollands is also known as Jenever, or Dutch

gin. A juniper-flavoured liquor drunk widely here in the Netherlands and Belgium. By grey-haired old ladies and alcoholics!"

Quince smiles: "I've never heard of it."

"That's because I've never bought it for you. It's disgusting. Worse than Grappa. My wife loves it. Although she is neither of the above."

"I know she isn't, Cas. I've met her many times."

The waiter suddenly cuts in: "Haring Hollandse Nieuwe, Paul."

Van Wijk agrees: "Ah yes, Jasper said he also ordered herring, one of the most famous Dutch dishes. The raw herring is normally served with chopped onions and gherkins. The customer wanted neither, just potatoes. Also, Jasper thought it was odd to order red wine with herring. It would normally be beer or white wine."

Quince addresses Jasper and Paul: "We understand Mr Flower left his iPhone at the Tulip and went to get it. Which way did he leave? Can you remember?"

Jasper makes a stab at some English: "He sat at a table over there. And is leaving - here." He points at the door that leads to hotel reception and outside..

Quince follows his line: "And he never came back?"

Jasper shakes his head, but Paul answers: "No. Jasper reported the matter to me. I waited a day or so and then I called Cas."

Cas looks at Quince: "I think we're done here, Quince. Let's go; unless you fancy herring?"

Quince smiles charmingly at Paul: "No, but I'd love a Dutch Kroket?" The Kroket is a deep-fried roll with meat ragout inside and covered with breadcrumbs.

Paul is impressed: "Yes and some Stroopwafel to go with your afternoon English tea. Of course. We'll fix you a takeaway."

"Thank you," says Quince. "My mouth is already watering!"

Beursplein

Amsterdam, Holland

QUINCE AND CAS VAN DER MAAS are in the underground car park near Warmoesstraat where Jax had left Andrew's Audi. It's in front of them.

Quince says: "But we come back to the same question. Why would a rich man with a nice car like this and a very attractive wife suddenly disappear? It doesn't make any sense."

"What's she like?" Cas is intrigued because he realises how much trouble Quince has taken to help her.

Quince considers: "She lacks the exuberance I would associate with most of the Americans I've met. When I say met – I mean encountered – on the beat in Parnell Square, Dublin. But they were on holiday, so they would be exuberant, I suppose."

"I see, ja, tourists."

"In fact, to answer your question more accurately, I'd say Mrs Flower was fragile." He pauses for a moment to choose his words carefully. "One of life's victims, as my mother used to say. Plenty of money ... but unhappy. There you have it, Cas."

"This is why you are helping her?"

Quince says nothing, but nods. He's said all he needs to.

"Ok, I understand." Cas hands Quince a piece of paper: "These are the travel details from the airport, by the way. Flower was booked on a flight from Schiphol to Miami via Frankfurt. But, as we now know, never turned up. We've rechecked all the hospitals and district police forces in Holland. Nothing at all."

Quince glances at the note: "Thanks, Cas. Keep me posted."

"Of course. He's probably found a nice Dutch girl and is hiding up in Alkmaar. That's what I would do."

"Alkmaar?"

"Yes. I wouldn't hang around in Amsterdam with me looking for him. Somebody knows where he is, Quince. Somebody always does. I must go and report back to Joop van Durren. He has bees in his barnet about budgets. So, I will go! Tot ziens!"

*

Quince unlocks the Audi with the keyfob Jacqueline had given him. He lifts the tailgate of the boot and loads Andrew's personal effects from the Dam Square Inn: the Louis Vuitton suitcase and matching suit carrier. They are now ready to return to Jacqueline as he promised. He pulls the cover over for safety.

He then sits in the driver's seat and makes himself comfortable - absorbing every detail of the Q4; trying to familiarise himself with the instruments and programming the Satnav for the journey back to the Hoek van Holland ferry port. He starts the car and something catches his eye, poking out of the bottom of the sun visor: Andrew Flower's Stena Line ferry ticket.

STENA LINE FERRY.

Departure Date/Time: 13. 06. 22. 23.00HRS

Route: HARWICH-HOEKVHOL (ONE WAY)

Vehicle Type: Audi saloon.

Number of Passengers: 1

Lead Name: Mr. Andrew Flower

UK Passport checked/ Checked in 13.06.22.

Quince says to himself out loud: "One way ... so he never had any intention of returning to England. Of that there is now no doubt." He pockets the ferry ticket and pulls out of the underground car park onto Beursplein; the journey home awaits him.

Triumph

Brook House, Salhouse, Norfolk, England

THE TRIUMPH TR4A sports car swings into the driveway. Jax is driving, headscarf and glasses. The roof is down, and the engine sounds throaty. She presses a remote control. The garage door tilts open. She glances inside: cars draped in protective dust covers. And on the walls of the garage commemorative competition plaques from Le Mans, Mille Miglia, Angoulême and Brands Hatch. There are benches, racks of tools, pots of oil and reels of cable. The paraphernalia of a devoted enthusiast.

She manoeuvres the car into a narrow space between an immaculate Citroën 2CV and a 1961 Facel Vega HK 500. Inside the TR, the discarded anniversary bow is a crumpled mess down in the passenger footwell along with the deflated balloons.

Jax takes her phone and scrolls to contacts: "Andrew. Can you please call me? It's been days. I'm – I'm worried." She hangs up, the record has been made. But for some reason she doesn't feel good about this particular piece of duplicity. She opens the door and struggles out of the tiny space between the Facel and the Citroën; she stretches and takes a few steps outside into the fresh air ...

*

She takes Andrew's phone out of her handbag and turns it on. She scrolls to *MISSED CALLS*, sees the American Miami number - 1 – 305 – 445 – 1926 - and calls it back

De Pablos answers.

"Mr De Pablos. This is Jacqueline Flower, Andrew's wife."

De Pablos sounds incredibly suspicious: "Finally a call. What is going on?"

"Andrew has been very ill in Holland."

"I see, what's wrong with him?"

She pauses: "Coronavirus. He's been isolated in a house near Amsterdam."

Silence. Jax persists: "Mr De Pablos?"

"Si ... yes?"

"The line went dead, I thought I'd lost you."

"If Andrew is ill in a house near Amsterdam, what are you doing with his phone?" His tone is suspicious.

Jax sighs; she has not expected such a shrewd response and is momentarily caught out: "He – Andrew – had it couriered back to the UK. He'll buy an American phone when he gets there, I guess." She gulps: will this stranger buy her thin story? She can hear the man's doubt.

"Mrs Flower. Your husband told my father you had separated. I'm sorry to say this. But we understood – quite clearly – he was divorcing you. How to say this in English – it was on the grounds of your infidelity – is that the word?"

My infidelity. Jax is shocked and hurt: "We had s-separated, y-yes, it's true. But I would never cheat on my husband; it was all a misunderstanding. Everything is alright now. He'll be up and about in a few days. I'm sure."

"Your troubles are all behind you? Is that what you're saying, Mrs Flower? Is that what you want my father and me to believe? This is important."

Suddenly and without warning she bursts into tears; she cannot get the words out: "Yes ... it's ... true ... I would never ..." There is a long gap, Jax grips her phone, fighting hysterics.

"Mrs Flower ... I have upset you ... and I am sorry."

Her breaths are fast: "It's .... It's ok."

De Pablos is a gambler, he waits: "If you are back on friendly terms with your husband ..."

"Yes, what?"

"And he trusts you?"

"Yes."

"Then what is the name of the bank and the account number in Amsterdam? The one into which we paid ten million pounds deposit?"

Jax desperately delves into her bag for the three pages of computer printout she'd threatened Chase with. She struggles to get them out of the envelope.

Finally: *"ABN AMRO. Privilege account number 0272682368. Andrew and Christopher are the account holders."*

After an agonising break, De Pablos Jnr finally says: "Si. Si. This is okay. I will ask my father to amend the terms of the contract. But what you have told me must be confirmed by either Andrew or Christopher. Is that clear?"

"Yes."

"My father won't mind. He likes happy families Mrs Flower ... I am pleased your marriage problems are solved."

The line goes suddenly dead. Jax is still dumbfounded by Andrew's despicable allegation and slumps against the garage doorframe, crying her heart out. Ten minutes later, her face streaked with tears and smudged make-up, she walks towards the house, and flicks the remote. The cars vanish from view, but the memory of that conversation will stay with her forever.

*

At the bottom of the drive, across the road, the Peugeot rental car is parked up, empty. Back at the house, the front door closes.

Rossi

Quince's office, Bethel Street Police Station, Norwich

QUINCE SITS AT HIS DESK with his overnight bag on his lap. Superintendent Brian Cragg puts his head round the door. Obviously in a hurry.

"How was Holland?"

"It's all as Mrs Flower stated."

"She alright then."

"As far as I know. I'm taking the car back to her home later."

"What was it like?"

Quince smiles: "The car or the country?"

"Both, matey. Both."

"Fine."

"Good. Stay with it, Quince. Whatever you need."

"Thank you, appreciated."

With that Cragg is gone. A moment later Helen comes bounding in with a bundle of papers under her arm. Quince takes his passport and iPhone out of his bag, plonks them down onto his desk. From out of nowhere he produces a bunch of flowers and a box of Swiss chocolates.

She glances at the goodies: "Quince! Welcome back!"

"What's up then, young Rossi? Your little face tells me you've got some news? Good, I hope."

Helen selects a couple of documents: "Yes. You remember the newspaper article about Nigel Flower? The car crash? He was Andrew's half-brother. Apparently, Flower senior was a bit of a lad in his youth."

Quince smiles at the expression.

Quince flicks on his computer; finds the email from Cas and opens the attachment: the CCTV footage of Gravenstraat with Andrew Flower walking towards the Dam Square Inn. Quince recognises Flower from the wedding photograph: about forty with sandy-brown hair and a neatly-styled goatee beard; he wears aviator-style glasses with a silver frame. Quince can't help noticing the Louis Vuitton suitcase and matching suit carrier now stowed in the back of the Audi. The image feels vaguely surreal.

"Do I still have your attention, Quince?"

"Yes, Rossi. One hundred per cent."

"Are those gifts for me?" She says hopefully.

"Yes, Rossi."

"Where was I?"

"Flower senior was a bit of a lad?"

"Right, yes. Anyway, after he was killed, Nigel's widow Isabelle received a settlement. It was obviously meagre because she contested it in Court."

"And?"

"She failed. Lives in Germany now. Probably gave up trying. You know how it goes."

Quince stands up quickly and gathers his things together. "Yes, I know how it goes. Good. Keep digging. Now, let's get the Audi back to Mrs Flower. Follow me in the Renault."

"Yes, if you say so."

Quince picks up the phone. He scans his desk for the post-it note Mrs Flower wrote on. He locates it, and calls. The dialling tone continues until the answering service cuts in.

"Mrs Flower, it's Quince. I've got the car and other items. If you're not there, I'll pop the keyfob through your letterbox." There is a tinge of disappointment in his voice.

"Are those lovely tulips really for me, Quince?"

"Yes."

"And the chocolates?"

"Well, we'll have to see about that, Rossi."

Delivery

Brook House, Salhouse, Norfolk

ANDREW FLOWER'S AUDI Q4 and a battered Renault Clio arrive on the deserted Flower residence driveway. Quince gets out of the Audi, goes over to the front door and rings the bell. Its chime can be heard echoing within. There is no response. Quince goes back to the Audi, locks it and puts the keyfob through the letterbox.

Quince whispers to himself with a sigh: "Pity, I'd like to have seen you, Jacqueline." He walks over to the Clio where Rossi is waiting. A moment later it pulls out of the driveway.

Peugeot

Norwich Road, Salhouse, Norfolk

AT THE BOTTOM OF THE DRIVEWAY, across the road, the Peugeot rental car is parked up. Elisabeth Deluc is concealed in some bushes. And although it is getting dark, she has videoed the car delivery sequence as possible evidence. She returns to the Peugeot and sits behind the wheel. She punches numbers and starts speaking in rapid German.

On the passenger seat beside her is a red leather document folder.

WILHELM WEHRMANN & KURT WAGNER,
PRIVATE INVESTIGATORS,
AUGSBURGERSTRASSE, BERLIN, GERMANY.

The conversation is animated, but her tone remains resolute and adamant: "Yes, Herr Wagner, that is what I'm saying. Andrew Flower did not turn up at Schiphol as arranged. The police have returned his Audi to Brook House, the Flower residence in Salhouse, where I am now ... I'll have a look around. Report in later ... Be assured I will do everything I can legally do."

She suddenly pulls the phone away from her ear; evidently Herr Wagner is not a happy man.

Conjecture

Quince's office, Bethel Street Police Station, Norwich

QUINCE BECKONS Griffiths into his office.

"You don't need to see any credentials?" Griffiths asks Quince politely, aware of his rank and reputation in Norwich.

"No. My Sergeant has already told me who you are and what you want. And signed you in." Quince's hand reaches for the recording machine. "You don't mind if I record this, do you?"

"I'd rather you didn't. It's unofficial."

"I'd rather I did. I have a bad memory. Plus, for me, it is official."

"Very well then. You've been away, I hear. As you know, I telephoned yesterday to make an appointment to see you."

"Please do sit down," Quince is courteous. "Yes, investigating the disappearance of Andrew Flower."

Griffiths makes himself comfortable in the only chair not covered with files: "And has he ... disappeared? You're sure?"

"Yes. And there are no clues. He checked into the Stena Line

Terminal in Harwich last Monday. His passport was checked, and he was issued a boarding pass."

Quince rummages in his pocket and produces the ferry ticket. Griffiths sees it; says nothing.

"13. 06. 22. 23.00 HRS. Andrew Flower's Audi. This was the ferry ticket I retrieved from it ... do you want to see it."

"I can see it, thank you. And?"

Quince tosses the ticket down on his desk: "He checked into the The Dam Square Inn. Cas van der Maas of the Amsterdam Police emailed me the CCTV footage of Gravenstraat, where it's located."

Griffiths sighs: "I see."

"The hotel receptionist – Anna Brun – checked him in. He put his overnight things in the room. But never stayed the night. By all accounts ... he vanished."

"Who was the last person to see him?"

"The last *witness* was a waiter in Hulscher's restaurant, Amsterdam. Very chic."

Griffiths says: "I see, thank you. He pauses. "Tell me, do you think Mr Andrew Flower could have been having an affair?

The question catches Quince off-guard. But Griffiths knows the truth because Elisabeth has told him. That she was embroiled in an elaborate honeytrap; and Andrew had fallen for it.

Quince says innocently: "I don't know. Why would he?" The implication in his mind is: how could Andrew do better than Jacqueline?

Griffiths folds his arms guardedly: "I wouldn't know. Why

does anyone? Let's just suppose that he was planning to leave Jacqueline for someone else. Conjecture."

Quince doesn't like conjecture; he prefers facts.

Griffiths continues: "Let's just suppose Jacqueline found out he was cheating on her; she was so enraged she killed him in Holland." He pauses. "Hell hath no fury like a woman scorned."

"I don't think so, Mr Griffiths. She has alibis and there are independent witnesses."

Griffiths bites his lip: "I don't like her ... I have to say."

"Really? But just because you don't like her doesn't mean she went over to Holland and killed her husband. Now, if you don't mind, I have a lot of catching up to do."

Quince stands up and shows him the door.

"Don't be so sure of her innocence, DI Quince."

*

Quince wanders into the main office where he finds Mac and Helen huddled over a computer. Mac summons his attention with his hand:

"Sir. We've managed to cobble together various bits of CCTV surveillance footage. Have you got a moment to take a look?"

"Sure." Quince sits beside Helen, and they watch the screen: "Play on, McDuff. I've got sharp little eyes, you know."

Mac kicks off: "Right, here we are. The first section is from the A120 east – Parkeston Bypass – West Dock Road. Here's the Audi now approaching Harwich International."

"Pity it's dark," Quince says testily.

"Bear with, Guv," Helen replies.

"As you can now see – clearly – Andrew Flower's Audi approaching the motorists' check-in at the Stena Line booth with Flower's car in shot. Note the registration number AWF 444."

"Bound for the Hoek van Holland. Got it. Good job, Mac."

Helen takes over: "Next there's some freeze-frame shots from the Dorchester Hotel. Mrs Flower and her friend Lucia Paluzzi outside on The Rooftop Bar and Terrace. The next shot having dinner together at the Grill, and the last frame settling their bill at reception, Wednesday. All the frames are timed and dated as you can see."

"Yes," says Quince, standing up. "Useful."

Mac continues: "I've requested surveillance footage from Harrod's, and also the ...."

"Steady on, Mac. We're not studying Mrs Flower's social life. We're investigating the disappearance of her husband."

"Belt and braces, sir. That's what you always taught me."

"Did I really?" Quince responds. "How very profound I can be sometimes. Good work, both. Do what you have to do. I'll support."

As Quince is about to leave the office, Mac and Helen look at one another. Helen says: "I think that Hywel Griffiths character has unbalanced him."

"I heard that, Rossi," says Quince at the door. "I've got sharp little ears too."

"Yes, Guv," Rossi puts her hand up to her mouth, embarrassed.

Lay By

North Norfolk Coast

IT'S RAINING HARD; a wild wind buffets the old TR4A. Jax sits at the wheel, and she looks weary. She checks her voicemail.

Quince's voice: "... I'll pop the key fob through the letterbox"

She punches in a number: "Chase, I need to see you urgently ..." She winds down her side window slightly, takes a breath of cold sea air: "The police have collected the Audi from Holland." There is a brief silence as Fielding absorbs the news. "Griffiths is tightening the noose. I'll call you tomorrow. We need to make a plan, Chase. Speak soon."

Jax tries another number, which clicks to answerphone: "Quince, it's Jacqueline. Thank you for bringing the car back and for your help. I'm just up on the Norfolk coast in the TR. Not the ideal day for a drive in an old English sports car, but I needed a change ... speak to you soon." She hangs up, knowing she is waffling to a relative stranger.

*

Torrential rain pours down as the TR4A pulls into the driveway of Brook House. The security lights click on as the beam from her headlights sweep across the front of the house and activate the sensor.

*

At the bottom of the drive the Peugeot rental is parked up, unoccupied.

*

On the driveway and around the house, it is pitch black save for the security lights. Jax gets out of the car and runs towards the front door. A raw instinct immediately tells her something is not right. She pushes her key into the lock, the door swings open. She knows she locked it before she went out. Every nerve in her body tingles with the anticipation of danger.

Elisabeth

Brook House, Salhouse, Norfolk

INSIDE THE FRONT HALLWAY, Jax cautiously moves forward; looks around, picks up the Audi key fob from Quince and closes the front door with a gentle click. The hallway is in darkness save for the dim glow from a table lamp. She goes to a panel of light switches and flicks several of them. Nothing.

On the bottom step of the stairs, she sees half a dozen light bulbs. She advances warily towards the kitchen, scanning in every direction. No sound. She fumbles for the light switches and flicks them. Nothing, again. Just the light from another side lamp. There is no sign of a disturbance.

She creeps quietly towards the glass sliding doors which give access to the swimming pool complex. She stops and slides one panel across. The water in the pool is still. Her breaths are fast. She looks in every direction, gulping with fear; she feels there is someone there but sees nothing ...

She turns and reaches out to another panel of light switches and flicks them, the same response. The only light in the complex is from the underwater safety lights in the pool. She creeps back to the kitchen ...

*

On the kitchen island are a comprehensive array of kitchen utensils; and, above it, a cutlery rack. She creeps over and removes a Sakuto Japanese knife. Then a noise, the sound of soft footfalls as a figure comes into the half-light.

Jax screams.

Elisabeth Deluc stands there, framed within the kitchen doorway, partly in shadow and then slowly walks towards her. Jax grips the knife tightly, her eyes shining with fear.

Jax sees her more clearly: black blazer, blue Levi jeans, face in shadow: "W-Who are ... you?" She changes her grip on the knife. The Damascus steel blade gleams.

"You know who I am. Where is Andrew?"

Jax is totally incredulous: "What?"

"Where is he? Did you kill him?"

"No." Jax nervously swaps the knife from hand to hand, without losing eye contact.

Elisabeth smiles: "I think you did."

"Why?"

"Because you believed he was running away with me. To Miami, with the money. Somehow you found out."

"Weren't you running away?"

"No."

"Then what? Who are you?"

Elisabeth steps forward: “A private investigator working for Isabelle Flower in Berlin.”

Jax is even more incredulous now: “What?”

“Yes. Isabelle tried the British courts and got nowhere. Fielding and Andrew tricked her. That knife is making me nervous, Jacqueline. Put it back in the rack, please.”

Jax skirts around the kitchen island. She sounds terrified, despite the knife: “Tricked her, how?”

“Proved to her incompetent German lawyers that the company was insolvent. Falsified accounts. That’s the gist of it.”

“I don’t believe you.”

“That’s your choice. I know the Flower company sale is worth £100 million pounds. I am Isabelle’s last chance. She wants what she believes is her share, a percentage of it at least. Now, tell me where Andrew is ... if you didn’t kill him.”

“I don’t know.”

“The police are investigating his disappearance, Jacqueline. You reported it. They even brought his car back from Holland. I watched a detective deliver it.”

“Ha! You’re a burglar! You broke in! I’ll call the police - I could easily kill you.” Jax jabs at her with the knife, but the threat has no real substance.

“You’re welcome to try.”

There is an awkward silence as they look each other over, weighing up the situation. Jax stops and lowers her weapon. Now she is fascinated.

Jax: “Let me get this straight. You were, what, seducing my husband for ...”

"Evidence. Now please put the knife down."

Jax steps back and places the knife onto the kitchen island; it is dangerous and yet accessible.

"Up in the rack, Jacqueline, out of reach."

"Alright."

Elisabeth goes over to the utility cupboard and bends down, retrieving fuses from her jacket pocket.

"What are you doing?"

Elisabeth turns: "Replacing the fuses I took out earlier."

"And the light bulbs on the stair, was you?"

"Who else?"

"That's a neat trick."

"Not really. I had to leave you some light in the hallway, or you wouldn't have entered the house."

"You left the front door open."

"Of course."

The lights come on. Elisabeth produces the red leather document folder from her shoulder bag and places it on the counter. "These are the people I work for in Berlin and this is my – ja, collation of evidence."

WILHELM WEHRMANN AND KURT WAGNER,
PRIVATE INVESTIGATORS,
AUGSBURGERSTRASSE, BERLIN, GERMANY.

"Are you German?"

Elisabeth puffs: "No. I'm Belgian; from Bruges. My father is French and my mother, Swedish. There you have it. That's why I speak so many languages. Most of us do in Belgium. We have to."

"How did you meet my husband?"

"The American Bar at the Savoy. His favourite haunt. I had to stalk him for two days ... so, as I said, this is my evidence." Elisabeth pushes the document folder closer so Jax can see it clearly.

Jax reads the gold writing; still mystified: "What kind of evidence?"

"Shifting cash offshore to avoid corporation tax. Creating bad debts from suppliers who don't exist to make the company appear insolvent. Mr Griffiths has been very busy on my account, investigating .... It is amazing what a man like Andrew will divulge in bed."

Jax mulls it all over; it's exactly the sort of thing Chase would be skilful at. She listens as Elisabeth continues.

"Oh, and also proving Nigel Flower died because Andrew and Fielding sabotaged his car: cut a hole in the brake line of his 1964 MGB. Made to look like it had perished with wear."

"You can't be serious?"

"Andrew knows a lot about old cars, doesn't he? He's got garages full of them. And the right sort of tools. Your friend Lucia Paluzzi sold Nigel the car. Did you know that?"

Jax remembers the green MGB but has no idea Lucia supplied it. She says nothing.

*

Outside in the rear garden, a masked man in dark clothing creeps across the dark lawn. He is holding a handgun double-handed grip, close to the ground: a military-style assault.

*

Elisabeth joins Jax at the kitchen island and pulls up a stool. She opens the document folder: "The question remains, where is Andrew? What happened to him?"

"I told you I don't know."

Elisabeth suddenly sounds tired: "Alright, alright. At Schiphol Griffiths and I were waiting. Andrew never showed. Vanished the night before in the Damrak area. In this folder, I have a copy of the Juan de Pablos contract. Andrew gave me a copy. Everything to do with the sale is in here."

"So, what's next?" Jax tries to hide her alarm at the level of his treachery against her.

"The police. But I am still puzzled. I spoke to Andrew personally at the Flower Company that Friday night. June 10th. On his mobile."

"Yeah, our wedding anniversary."

Elisabeth looks at her: "I arranged to meet him at the Lufthansa check-in desk at Schiphol the following Tuesday 14th. He had our tickets ... he never showed up ... but you did ... I'd like to know why."

"Me! Why would I go to Schiphol?"

"I don't know, but you recognised me, didn't you? I saw it in your eyes just now."

Jax is tired too. She knows the game is nearly up. Elisabeth throws down a couple of photos. Her ace stratagem: a woman holding a crash helmet. Shoulder-length frizzy red hair, tinted glasses. The Yamaha motorcycle: the famous Spanish dancer. It's her as clear as day. Jax freezes.

"Motorway services, Amsterdam A2 South, I believe."

Jax stares at the photos, horrified.

Elisabeth picks one up: "Hywel Griffiths is a better tax inspector than he is a photographer, but I can see from your face that you get the picture."

A long silence. Elisabeth stares at Jax. A wry smile: "And I don't find him Very Irrésistible, do you? Quite the reverse, but good at his job. What do they say – a number cruncher – yes?"

Jax is caught, trapped. After all her scheming and plotting she has been outmanoeuvred by that bully Griffiths. He's been ahead of her all the time. There is nothing she can do now.

One last pitch from Elisabeth: "What were you doing in Holland, Jacqueline? Just tell me the truth. Whatever it is, is over."

Slowly, very slowly, Jax inches nearer to the kitchen island again, edging towards the knife rack. She can't give up now; she's contemplating using the knife. A last resort. Elisabeth's expression flickers in realisation. A momentary hesitation.

Jax sees and tries to distract her: "I've – I've never been to Holland."

With a quick, well-executed movement Jax makes to grab the knife. She's there, touching it. At that very moment there is a loud smash of glass from somewhere outside. They look at one another in shock. The kitchen door opens.

The masked man enters silently. Black trousers, black jacket, black trainers. Two cold eyes stare out at them both through narrow slits in the mask. He's holding the weapon; double-handed grip.

Jax suddenly stands up, turns to Elisabeth and screams: "Jacqueline! Get down! Get down!"

Elisabeth is visibly puzzled and stands up from the kitchen stool, confused. The gunman raises his arm, takes aim carefully and then pumps six silenced rounds into Elisabeth's body.

Explosions of red erupt all over her blazer like tiny volcanoes and she falls, screaming loudly to the floor, clutching her chest. It takes seconds to happen. Jax throws herself to the ground as one shot goes wide. It sears through the air and hits a large white dresser several feet behind her.

That single shot hits a large yellow vase on one of the wooden shelves. It shatters with the impact of the bullet, exploding like a bursting light bulb. Glass, fragments of porcelain and tiny chips of wood spray out into the room. On her hands and knees, she crawls through the debris. Her bare skin is pressing down onto the shards of broken glass and china.

Behind, the masked gunman moves towards her, his weapon still hot. The sudden shock of the vase exploding has distracted him too, just for a second. It is enough. Jax leaps up and runs towards the swimming pool complex.

*

For a few seconds the pool looks blue, calm and shimmering. Then the sliding doors to the complex shatter as Jax charges through them towards the pool's edge.

The intruder is right behind her now. A second later his arms are around her knees in a flying rugby tackle. She crashes down to the ground on her stomach, her elbows taking most of the impact. The impetus makes them both slide along to the edge of the pool, slipping around uncontrollably on the tiles. Jax tries to scream. He flips her over onto her back. His hands grab her throat, compressing her windpipe with his thumbs, throttling her. His strength is unrelenting, she's choking to death.

The intruder's masked face is inches away from hers: "Die bitch. Die."

She retches; the pain is unbearable. She struggles, trying to pound his chest, suddenly an opportunity as his legs part: she knees him in the groin. Hard. He winces with pain; and in that split second, she drives her middle finger right into his eye with all the force she can summon. He screams in agony. He relaxes his grip on her. His hand shoots to his eye defensively. But it's too late. She's pierced through his eyeball with her fingernail. right up to her knuckle. Aqueous and vitreous fluid spill out onto her hand.

For seconds they wrestle and roll into the pool. His ruined eye bleeds into the water: He's yelling "I – can't – s-swim." He's gulping for breath, his injury hideous.

Jax swims away from him. The intruder thrashes around,

helpless. He goes under; then his head rises out of the water, his face white, the eye wound oozing:

"Fucking help me."

Jax screams at him: "Who hired you?"

The intruder's struggling, lungs filling with water.

"Tell me."

"Flower ... Fl ..."

She sobs: "Oh, Jesus. No. No. No."

The dead figure sinks to the bottom of the pool, leaving a trail of bubbles and blood. Jax swims over to the side of the pool, hauls herself out, panting, sobbing with the realisation that Andrew had sent the man to murder her, but had got Elisabeth instead.

Finally, she rolls over onto her side, shaking. After a few minutes she struggles up onto all fours and slowly stands ...

It takes her twenty minutes to finally compose herself. She walks unsteadily to the changing room and finds herself a pair of rubber flip-flops; then makes her way towards the space where the sliding door had been. There are shards of safety glass everywhere. She steps walks through the space, looking back once more at the body in the pool.

*

In the kitchen, Jax finds Elisabeth lying on the floor in a crumpled, broken heap. Her eyes are still open and seem to be staring up in total disbelief at her own sudden horrific death.

There is debris all around her from the gun shots. She bends over and picks out Elisabeth's phone and keyfob for the Peugeot from the mess on the floor. She takes them both over to the kitchen sink and washes them under hot running water – lets the tap run for a few minutes to thoroughly clean the basin - then dries the two items on kitchen roll. She gathers all the documents and two photos from the kitchen island and puts them into Elisabeth's shoulder bag, with the phone and keyfob. She takes the flip-flops off at the kitchen doorway and walks barefoot towards the carpeted dining room; mindful not to leave bloody footprints on the beige Wilton.

*

On the wall is an oil painting of a very rare Bugatti; it is hinged to one side like a door. Concealed behind it is a large capacity Chubb safe. Jax swings the painting open and taps in the 8-digit pin code onto the digital keypad and the safe door pops open. She takes Elisabeth's shoulder bag full of incriminating evidence and stows it safely away. She shuts the safe door with a decisive clunk, re-sets the code and swings the painting back in place. She goes back to the kitchen doorway and puts the blood-stained flip-flops back on.

Once in the kitchen, she picks up the landline and dials 999.

Visitor

Cathedral Close, Norwich

THE RAIN OUTSIDE QUINCE'S BEDROOM window is pounding, but he doesn't hear it, he sleeps so deeply. Suddenly there is a thunderous knock on the front door. Quince is out of bed in a second and runs down the stairs to answer it ...

Mac is standing there. Behind him in the Close is a police car; blue flashing light and hazards.

Quince rubs his eyes: "Mac ... what's up?"

"It's Mrs Flower, Guv. She's been attacked at her house. Two dead, a man and a woman."

Quince is visibly shaken. Suddenly nothing else matters: "Attacked? Is she alright, Mac?"

"Come and see. She asked for you. I've sent for the cavalry. They're on their way to Brook House now."

Quince immediately pounds up the stairs: "Three minutes, Mac. All I need."

Crime Scene

Brook House, Salhouse, Norfolk

THE KITCHEN IS BUZZING WITH CSI - Crime Scene Investigators - dressed in pastel-coloured overalls, gloves and facemasks. An investigator removes Elisabeth's jewellery, including a silver bracelet. The evidence is meticulously bagged. Finally, her corpse is lifted into a body bag and zipped up with brisk, impartial formality. Blood swabs and fibres are being taken from the walls and kitchen floor; plus, extensive photos of the crime scene from all angles. It is a hive of practised activity – the silent team know what to do.

The intruder's bloody firearm is retrieved from the kitchen floor and placed in an evidence bag by an investigator. A Glock 17M.

"It's lighter than normal, because rounds have been spent," the detective says knowingly.

*

In the swimming pool complex, Jax is sitting on the floor,

cross-legged, still in wet clothes. Mac, WPC Helen Ross remain standing, while Quince is sitting on a garden chair.

He addresses Jax with genuine concern: “What happened, Jacqueline?”

Jax’s face is a blank, her eyes still shining with fear. In her mind, all she can think of is her spontaneous warning to Elisabeth: ‘Jacqueline! Get down! Get down!’. Then the dull thump of six gunshots. And the man ...

She swallows: “I - I came back here from a drive along the coast. Called you. Left a message ...I don’t know if you got it ...”

Quince nods, looks at the others as she continues: “The house was in darkness, front door was open, so I knew there was an intrusion. I was frightened, but I let myself in. He – he had just shot that woman in the kitchen. So, so, quick. Then he turned. And saw me ... it was ...”

*

At the swimming pool, the intruder’s corpse is being lifted out by two CSI; they are careful and well-practised.

CSI ONE is in the pool in a wet suit. CSI TWO is at the side in forensic overalls. The corpse is placed onto a large, plastic sheet.

CSI TWO produces a digital fingerprint scanner from an SOC bag. It looks like a mobile phone with a wire from the bottom of it that leads to a small finger-sized scanner. The intruder’s right hand is carefully dried, the thumb is placed against the screen and gently pressed down.

A third CSI is taking swabs of blood, fluid and tissue from the eye socket; plus, saliva. Also hair samples. Photos of the corpse and pool are being taken by another CSI.

CSI TWO: “Sent. Fast track. Fifteen minutes and we’ll know who he is.”

CSI ONE: “If he’s on a fingerprint database.”

The third CSI says: “This is a professional killer, not a random break in.”

*

Quince, Mac and Helen wait. Jax is visibly distraught.

Quince says softly: “And then?”

Jax continues: “I ran from the kitchen to here, alongside the pool. He chased after me. Pushed me down to the ground, like a rugby tackle. Then he was strangling me ... I couldn’t breathe ... fingers pressed into my throat ...” She cries out: “He was trying to kill me ... I – I lashed out at him. Somehow, I got away and we ended up in the pool. I don’t remember how.”

CSI ONE comes over with a small case, addresses Quince: “Sir, sorry. We’ll need the usual.”

Quince moves closer to her: “Jacqueline, we’ll need to scrape your fingernails for forensic samples. DNA. Blood and tissue. It’s procedure.”

Jax looks at him, her eyes blurry with tears: “Sure.”

“And WPC Ross will also need your clothes for Forensics to look at. They’ll be a second chaperone. It’s your right.”

CSI TWO, with gloved hands removes samples of blood, tissue, fluid and fibres from Jax’s fingernails and places them in little evidence bags. Another CSI takes photos of the injuries to Jax's neck and throat. The flashes of light illuminate the complex like lightening. Jax blinks, traumatised by the police activity.

*

In the bedroom suite Jax, WPC Ross and a female CSI chaperone walk into the adjoining dressing room. A paper sheet is laid down for Jax to stand on. Jax undresses slowly and drops all her clothes into separate paper evidence bags which are being held open for her by the officers. There is no contact.

Helen is watching Jax: "You've been through something awful here tonight, Mrs Flower. What you did to defend yourself ..."

"I had no choice, did I?" Jax says shakily. "My life was at risk. He would have killed me ... that was for certain ... I was attacked as a young teenager in the States. I'll never forget the terror I suffered. And I felt the same terror again this evening. I hope I can recover." She pauses. "I'm sorry, I shouldn't load you with my gruesome history."

"That's fine, Mrs Flower," Helen says with heartfelt sympathy. "It sounds terrible. I really feel for you. Honestly."

There is an awkward moment. Then Helen notices the framed film posters: Mrs Doubtfire; Sliding Doors; Tootsie. She needs to try and change the subject; the chaperone picks up and gives Helen an encouraging look.

"You obviously like films, Mrs Flower? Or should I say movies?"

"Yeah, I used to do a bit of acting ... but that was a long time ago. Those are just a few of my favourite movies."

"Mine too."

Jax brightens up: "The 'Tootsie' poster is signed by Dustin Hoffman and Sydney Pollack who directed it."

Helen goes over, looks at the poster, sees the autographs: "Wow!" She says, impressed.

"Of course, Sydney Pollack produced 'Sliding Doors.' That's the movie where Gwyneth Paltrow plays Helen, two versions of the same girl ... great acting."

"Helen?" says Helen with a grin.

"Right! The one who did get on the tube-train and the one who didn't ... which was real?" Jax says. "That's the question, I guess."

"I reckon you were a little more than a bit part actor, Mrs Flower."

"Not really ... boy, I'm getting cold. Can I get dressed?" Jax is regaining her self-control.

Helen persists politely: "You certainly know a lot."

"I had a few lucky breaks, I guess. I'm shivering ..."

At that moment a Paramedic steps into the room, wearing overshoes and with a kitbag slung over her shoulder. She's thirties, bright and breezy, reassuring: "Just a few minutes, then you can get dressed, Mrs Flower. I need to check you over. Alright?"

Jax nods: "I'll get my gown. I hope you've warmed up your stethoscope!"

Helen laughs: she likes Mrs Jacqueline Flower: there is

obviously a lot more to her than meets the eye.

*

Back in the swimming pool complex CSI TWO approaches Quince who is still sitting on the garden chair, laptop on his knee, waiting for results.

Behind him, the body bag containing the corpse of the intruder is being lifted onto a trolley.

The investigator coughs judiciously: "Police national computer / NT negative, sir."

Quince huffs: "No trace, eh? That's bloody inconvenient."

CSI TWO shows Quince the fingerprint scanner and he can see the image of a thumbprint – a conflation of black curves and swirls on a green screen – with the date and exact time.

Jax and Helen approach them. Jax is now wearing her white dressing gown, with her hair wrapped up like a turban, the way she does.

Quince stands courteously: "Ah! Good. Where would you like to stay tonight? This house is now a crime scene, I'm afraid and obviously out of bounds."

Jax summons a vague smile: "Lucia. I sent her a text. She'll look after me."

Helen turns to Quince: "The Paramedic has examined Mrs Flower, Guv. Nothing broken. She doesn't need hospital. And we have everything we need. For now."

Quince says: "Mrs Flower, we can't force you to go to hospital if you're sure you are alright. You know, if the Paramedic has signed you off, as it were."

She nods: "I'm ok, thank you. I need a Jack Daniels for medicinal purposes, you understand?"

Quince smiles warmly, his eyes twinkle: "I'm sure you do. We'll need a statement, Mrs Flower. Can we drive you to Lucia's home afterwards?"

"Lucia is on her way, but thanks anyway. You've all been so kind."

But Quince does become suddenly formal: "I'm going to place you under Police protection at Lucia's. You are a witness to a brutal murder. Don't worry though, you won't even know my officer is there."

Jax nods: "Sure, thanks."

*

A short time later, Quince, Rossi and Mac stand in the driveway of Brook House in drizzling rain. It is a moment that will always be imprinted on their minds. The Paramedic stands in the doorway, filling in a form. Lucia is walking with Jax away from the house towards the VW Karmann Ghia. Jax, wrapped up in a blanket, moves slowly. Lucia starts the engine, and the car is gone. The security lights are still on, bleaching the driveway with their glare. The Audi and the TR4A are shiny with rain. The scene is surreal: a number of police officers remain to guard the taped-off crime scene. The house which still looks so majestic has become the centre of killing and bloodshed.

Old Windmill

Norfolk Broads, Norfolk

LUCIA'S HOME, AN OLD WINDMILL, sits beside the Norfolk Broads and is picture- perfect. Set within two acres of gardens, it overlooks the water.

Inside, it is chock-a-block with paraphernalia: paintings, sketches, and drawings adorn every conceivable space. Italian opera spills discreetly from smart speakers and the lighting is soft. The old mill creaks as every piece of wood is challenged by the wind.

Lucia and Jax are nursing brandy balloons. The scene should be cosy and relaxed, except Jax has something on her mind: "Did you sell Nigel the green MGB he died in?"

Lucia is suddenly alarmed: "Yes, yes, I did. Why?"

"Elisabeth told me. Why did you never tell me?"

"I thought I did."

"No, Lu. You never did. Well?"

Lucia shakes her head and takes a slug of brandy: "Nigel and I had a brief affair. Nothing serious."

"While he was still married to Isabelle, you mean?"

"Yes."

"Why didn't you tell me about that either? I thought we were friends?"

Lucia stands and wanders over to the satin walnut Georgian drinks cabinet: "This is Vecchia Romagna, Italian brandy. It's supposed to be served with after-dinner chocolates." She holds up the crystal decanter. "But I don't have any. You want another?"

"No. Why didn't you tell me?"

"Andrew – Andrew told me not to."

"Andrew! Why would he care?" Jax is more than surprised. She's mystified.

"I don't know."

"Yes, you do, Lu. Quit bullshitting me. It doesn't suit you."

Lucia returns to her seat, can't make eye contact: "Because ... Andrew, Nigel and I had a threesome."

Jax laughs in sheer disbelief: "What? Like a sexual threesome?"

"You're not that naïve, Jax. Yes."

Jax swigs her brandy and almost chokes.

"It only happened a few times. Often when Andrew had cocaine to share."

"Cocaine? What! ... I can't believe I'm hearing this ... Andrew. He wasn't the type for cocaine."

"Yes, he was ... I'm sorry; I knew him long before you came on the scene, Jax."

"I know that. But how come I remember the green MGB

then? And Nigel dying in it, more's the point. This is just not right. I suddenly feel dirty."

Lucia remains silent.

"Is this why you're helping me? The whole deception thing – to assuage your guilt?"

Finally, Lucia looks at Jax: "No." She pauses. "I'm doing it because I am very fond of you. You know that."

Jax holds out her glass, sounding unconvinced: "Oh really. I guess I will have another drink, after all, small one."

Lucia silently replenishes her glass and Jax nods: "Well, well. This day doesn't get any better, does it? I'm attacked by a fucking masked gunman ... and then discover my best friend has screwed my husband."

"It's not like that, Jax."

"Yeah? How is it then, huh? Explain to me how it's not like that!"

The sound of Giacomo Puccini plays in the background and Lucia is at a loss for words; the tension between them is unbearable. Jax knocks back her drink in one gulp.

"There's something else, Jax. More serious. Which is why I never told you."

"I can't wait."

"Andrew found out that Nigel secretly filmed at least one of these – events – and Nigel tried to blackmail him."

Jax's mind is in a whirl as she considers: "Wait a minute ... blackmail him for what? Nigel didn't need money; he inherited from his father's estate. Half a mill. I remember."

Lucia knows more: "Yes, but they were half-brothers. Nigel

wasn't a shareholder of the Flower Group; maybe he wanted shares and Andrew refused to part with them. Five hundred thousand pounds isn't that much in comparison. I don't really understand such business matters. I'm clearly just a simple car trader."

"Clearly." Jax's tone is loaded with sarcasm. Her head slumps onto the back of the chair. She recalls the conversation she'd had with Elisabeth and the reason why Isabelle hired Wehrmann and Wagner in the first place:

'Oh and proving Nigel Flower died because Andrew and Fielding sabotaged his car. Tampered with the brake cable on a 1964 MGB. Your friend Lucia Paluzzi sold Nigel the car. Did you know that?'

No, she damn well didn't know that. But she does now. She wonders what other secrets Elisabeth has in her notebook.

She sighs, exasperated and fixes Lucia with an accusing stare: "Did Isabelle Flower find out about this business with Andrew and Nigel? The threesome. The blackmail for shares? Is this what started her vendetta against Andrew in the first place? Isabelle is convinced Andrew killed Nigel. Is this why? Is there anything more you are not telling me?"

"I don't know, Jax. That's the honest truth. All I did was sell Nigel the car."

"Was there anything wrong with it?"

"Like what?"

"Dodgy brakes for a start. What was the East Anglian Daily Times headline – 'Local businessman killed in puzzle car accident' - Four years ago. I remember it all now, so I was on the scene, as you put it. The accident happened on the Norwich Ring Road near Grapes Hill. 'The likely cause was a split in the brake line; the hydraulic fluid leaked out. The split may have been due to wear.' That's what the article said: may have been. Boy oh boy. I'm tempted to ring Isabelle Flower and ask what she thinks. Her Berlin telephone number is in Elisabeth's folder, so's her mobile."

"I wouldn't do that, bella."

"Why not?"

"Because we are both trying to perpetuate the belief that Andrew is alive in Holland. Not crushed to death in his own meat processing plant ..."

Jax ponders: "Maybe."

"Plus, it might point the finger at you, and you can't take any chances. Not now. Leave Isabelle alone, Jax. We're still not through this." Lucia sees Jax is warming to her point of view.

"Yeah, ok. You're right, I guess." She stalls ... "You're still gonna help me, right?"

"Si, I am still going to help you ... Can you manage a drop more Vecchia, Jax?".

"No. I'm going to go out and get some fresh air, have a wander by the water and contemplate. Then I'm gonna come in, drink some water, take two paracetamol, a sleeping tablet and nestle under the duvet in your spare bedroom ... and forget the world until I wake." She stands, rubs her hands, decision made.

"Certo ... of course." Lucia judiciously waits a few seconds. "I don't know what to say to you about what happened, Jax."

"Then say nothing. Always best."

Revelation

The Flower Group Car Park, Norwich

CHRISTOPHER FIELDING WALKS from the car park to the front entrance of the plant. Quince and Mac approach him, both proffering their Police ID.

Quince: "Mr Fielding? A quiet word please? Norfolk Constabulary, CID."

Fielding stops, glances at his Rolex, surprised: "Well, yes. Of course. How can I help you?"

"You are Mr Andrew Flower's lawyer?"

Fielding smiles: "Yes. Yes. Company lawyer. Fellow director and, friend I would hope. Is there something wrong?"

Mac: "Yes, very much so. Mrs Flower was attacked last night at her home. The intruder tried to kill her."

Fielding is visibly shaken: "What? Is – is – she – alright? Is – ?"

Quince answers: "Remarkably, yes. It's a terrible shock for you, we can see that. But have you any idea who might wish to harm her?"

Fielding says: "You mean, it wasn't an armed robbery? When you used the word intruder, I assumed you meant a burglary?"

Quince is straight in: "Based on the information we have, a man – with a gun – broke into Brook House, killed a woman and then tried to kill Mrs Flower. We have no ID on the other woman."

Fielding is aghast: "God. Not Lucia?"

"No. Not Mrs Paluzzi," Quince says reassuringly.

Mac points at the door of the plant: "Would it be better to go inside, Mr Fielding?"

"Yes, come up to the conference room. Quieter there."

*

Fielding, Quince, and Mac are sitting around the conference table. Fielding has his suit jacket off and looks uncomfortable.

Quince: "So, you have no idea who might want to harm Mrs Flower? Business rivals? Anyone at all?" He pauses. "Such a vicious crime is unheard of in this neck of the woods."

"No."

"I see," Quince says. "You are aware Andrew has been reported missing by Jacqueline? Five days now."

Fielding nods, non-committal, but there is something in his eyes.

Mac: "The situation has now escalated, given the time frame. Could be suicide, sudden death somewhere, or even murder. We just don't know." Mac's words are well and carefully chosen. He and Quince had been over their approach on the way over.

Quince continues:

"No phone or email activity. No credit cards used for over five days. As far as we know, and from speaking to Mrs Flower, he is not a user of social media ..."

"Facebook? No! Not Andrew. Far too common; all one's secrets aired in public."

"Therefore, Andrew went totally off the radar somewhere in Amsterdam. Thoughts, Mr Fielding?"

"Andrew has been seeing someone over in Holland. German, I think. Maybe Dutch."

Quince: "Man? Woman?"

"I don't know her name and I've never met her. I don't - don't – wish to. I find the whole thing most distasteful."

Mac jumps in: "Has he done this before? Vanished like that?"

Fielding leans forward again, places his hands on the table: "Many times; on the pretext of business. I disapprove of his, his, well, philandering. Andrew is a compulsive character: women and cars. Sex and the evil white powder. He drains the company of cash. And me, of patience." He pauses and regards his two visitors. "There, I have said it."

Quince and Mac exchange glances, this is a revelation. Not the Andrew they had imagined.

Fielding carries on: "So, when you ask me if I am aware he is missing, then yes, I am. But five days is longer than usual, I must admit."

Fielding stands and goes to the bar and lifts a bottle of Evian, offering his visitors a drink. Mac and Quince decline so he pours himself a glass.

"Yes, well this time Andrew says it's serious."

Mac: "Sounds a complicated man, Mr Flower."

Fielding raises his eyebrows: "Complicated? Yes, that's one word to describe him."

"Could Jacqueline's attacker at Brook House be connected to this affair in Holland? A jealous husband or ex-lover?"

Fielding considers: "I'd doubt it. It's a big house in a remote part of Norfolk. They're wealthy, let's face it. And possible targets for crime. Sorry I can't be of more help."

Quince suddenly stands; Mac follows suit: "You've been very helpful. Thank you, Mr Fielding."

Fielding says: "I'm devastated about Jacqueline. I hope you discover who this attacker is. You didn't say if he had been arrested or not, DI Quince?"

Quince chooses to ignore the question: "We'll see ourselves out, Mr Fielding. Oh, we'll need a statement. My colleague here will be in touch. One last thing; can you account for your movements over the last week or so?"

Fielding picks up a leather desk diary: "It's all in here, gentlemen. No secrets."

As soon as they leave, he takes out his phone and scrolls to contacts: Lucia.

Thirty-Six Hours Later

Bethel Street Police Station. Brian Cragg's Office. Norwich

CRAGG, QUINCE AND HELEN ROSS are assembled in the sitting area of Cragg's immaculate office.

Cragg kicks the meeting off: "So how is Mrs Flower? You have a statement?

Helen nods and passes Cragg a plastic wallet which denotes: 'Witness Statement.'

Quince: "Nasty-looking bruising to her neck and throat area."

"What about hospital? Why wasn't she admitted?"

Helen responds: "She didn't want to be, sir. The Paramedic checked her over soon after the attack happened and was fine with Jacqueline going to Lucia's."

Cragg opens another Norfolk Constabulary/CSI folder and carefully removes various reports and photographs: "Right then. CSI have made their observations. No lead on the dead woman yet. We've checked with the Interpol fingerprint database. And FBI. Now, have a look at this, Quince."

Cragg hands Quince the folder. He reads it out loud: "'The bruising on Mrs Flower's neck and throat are entirely consistent with an attempted strangulation. The intruder fired six rounds in all. The weapon and spent cartridges were bagged and retrieved from the crime scene.'"

"Sounds good," says Quince.

"Yes," Cragg replies. "And they are being sent to NABIS, the ballistics intelligence service. See if we can get a link to other crimes. Oh, I gather you've found a stolen motorbike, WPC Ross?"

Helen: "Yes, sir. A Suzuki recovered a short distance away. Stolen from Paddington. Most probably the intruder's method of transport. We're checking the owner's records."

Cragg eyes the assembled group: "How did the dead woman get to Brook House? It is quite remote. Any vehicles unaccounted for?" They all shake their heads, a notion not considered. "Anything more?"

"Mac is going to take a formal statement from Christopher Fielding," says Quince. "He's the company's lawyer. Everything he told us about Andrew Flower. Mick, the factory foreman, has given us a sworn statement too. He saw Mr and Mrs Flower on Friday 10th June; she came to collect her husband at the meat processing plant here."

Cragg sniffs: "And Flower has still not shown up anywhere on the grid, I assume?"

Quince glances at Helen: "No, sir. Mrs Flower has heard nothing. He's gone to ground in Holland. Possibly with another woman, if what Fielding told us is accurate. A serial womaniser is how he described Flower."

Cragg turns the corners of his mouth down: "Are we assuming – from what we know – that Flower arranged to have his wife killed, murdered, while he is AWOL in Holland? Good God."

Quince: "That's certainly how it looks to me, yes. Fielding has painted us a pretty disturbing image of the real Andrew Flower. We need to speak to Jacqueline's friend, Lucia Paluzzi. She's next on the agenda."

Cragg stands; the meeting is over: "Good. We have Mrs Flower's statement and the CSI Report. But we'll need follow-up on her injuries. Mac, get Fielding's statement pronto. Keep me posted, Quince. Thank you, all."

Buongiorno

The Old Windmill, Norfolk Broads

QUINCE AND HELEN ROSS STAND outside Lucia's windmill. The front door opens, and Lucia appears, bright and breezy: "Buongiorno!"

"I'm DI Quince and this is my colleague, WPC Helen Ross, Norfolk Constabulary, Bethel Street." He has ID in his hand, but Lucia shakes her head as if to say: I don't need to see it.

"Yes, I got your message. Please to come in." Lucia is wearing a cropped medusa cardigan over a white silk blouse and a pair of black pleated georgette pario trousers by Versace. The shoes are Gucci. She beckons them in.

Quince says: "This is a fabulous spot, Mrs Paluzzi. It reminds me of Skerries in County Dublin, very picturesque."

"Grazie." Lucia gives them both a delightful, welcoming smile which reveals perfect teeth: "Please to follow me."

*

Quince and Helen follow Lucia into the lounge and admire

the understated class of her furnishings. Car magazines adorn a coffee table. Classic FM plays quietly in the background and there is an aroma of freshly ground coffee in the air.

"How is Mrs Flower today?" Quince breaks the ice.

There is a moment of hesitancy: "She's so so. She's at her doctor's surgery."

Lucia invites them both to sit.

He cracks the ice further: "Mrs Paluzzi, have you any idea why Jacqueline should be targeted in such a way?"

Lucia's bright smile fades: "Targeted?"

"Someone tried to strangle her. You've seen the bruises. You saw the mayhem at the house last night."

Lucia nods vaguely and composes herself: "Yes. Of course, I did. Poor Jax."

Quince looks at Helen who is making notes: "What did the intruder want? That's the question I keep asking myself. Why was he there at all?"

Lucia: "I don't know. One of the cars, maybe?"

"Cars?"

Lucia lets the word sink in: "Andrew had quite a collection."

Quince frowns: "Had?"

"Has."

Quince can see it now, the possible motive: theft. But why did the intruder need a Glock 17M to steal a fancy motor? He waits as Lucia thinks.

She says: "The DB5 alone must be worth a million. Low mileage and completely original."

Helen looks at Quince, confused: "DB5 – what's that?"

"Aston Martin, like James Bond's motor. Odd then, he should disappear and leave such valuable possessions behind. Don't you think?"

Lucia smiles. A false smile. Something is not right about Mrs Paluzzi and her answers. So, he pushes her a bit harder.

"And he never even got to drive the TR4A you sold Mrs Flower."

Lucia is frantically trying to stay composed: "No. Not yet anyway."

Quince stands and Helen follows quickly, getting the message. "Anyway. My Dutch colleagues are a vigilant bunch. So, I'm sure we'll get to the bottom of this. Don't you, WPC Ross?"

"Yes, I certainly do, guv."

"There's nothing you wish to say, Mrs Paluzzi? Or to ask us?"

"No, I don't think so. What could there be?"

"Anything you can think of."

"No, I have told you all I know. Will I have to make a statement?"

"No," Quince says affably. "You weren't a material witness. Just look after your patient ... I'm sure you will."

"Jax is my best friend. I will care for her. Don't you worry."

"Good." A supposed afterthought: "Oh, yes. One last thing, Mrs Paluzzi ... a bit, ahm, delicate."

Lucia stares at Quince, raises her eyes as if to say 'yes' and also stands.

"Were they happily married; would you say? Andrew and Jacqueline? What do you think? You won't be being disloyal to her by confiding your thoughts. It will help. And it will go no further, I assure you."

Lucia waits: "Jax bought him a lovely car as an anniversary gift. A celebration of their relationship. So, I would say they were totally devoted, does that help, DI Quince?"

"Yes. Don't worry, we can see ourselves out, Mrs Paluzzi. Thanks for your time."

*

Outside, a few moments later, Quince turns to Rossi: "That wasn't a very convincing answer, was it? Given what we know about Mr Flower's escapades."

"No. And Mrs Paluzzi is preoccupied with something or other. I could see it in her eyes."

"Yes, and she fiddles with her hands a lot. Did you notice?"

"I did, Guv. Seeing as you mention it."

Aylsham

Market Square, Aylsham, Norfolk

SIMULTANEOUSLY, THE DUTCH RENTAL PEUGEOT is being parked up in Aylsham's Market Square. Jax walks away from the car, dumps the keyfob into a waste bin without stopping. She is wearing sunglasses, a black polo neck sweater, black jacket, and tight-fitting Levi jeans. The injuries to her neck are covered by the sweater. She walks across Market Square towards a waiting Daimler saloon.

Christopher Fielding gets out of the polished car as soon as he sees Jax. He is dressed in a flawlessly tailored raw-silk suit, blue shirt and Royal London Yacht Club tie. He epitomises panache but looks genuinely concerned as she approaches him.

"Jax. The police came to see me and told me what happened. Are you alright?" There is no offer of a cheek from her for their customary polite kiss.

"Not really, Chase. I'll just get in. We need to talk."

"Yes, you sounded anxious on the phone earlier."

He goes round to the passenger door and courteously opens

it for her. Jax gets in with obvious discomfort and removes her sunglasses. If he saw Jax park the Peugeot, he doesn't mention it. She settles in the passenger seat, while he gets in.

"What happened, Jax. Tell me."

"A thug broke into my house and tried to kill me. Andrew had hired him."

"You can't possibly be serious?"

"Do I look like I made it up?" She pulls down the roll of her sweater so he can see her neck: black and blue bruising. Her left eye is red and swollen. "I have more bruising on my shoulders and back. The guy tried his best to strangle me, Chase. He very nearly succeeded."

"Jesus."

"I'm gonna ask you this once. Did you know what Andrew had planned?"

Fielding turns and looks at her: "No."

"Sure, because if you did, I walk away now."

"No, I swear. No."

She breathes a sigh of relief: she wants to believe him; she needs to believe him. "Ok."

"How do you know for sure Andrew ...?" Fielding can't actually say the words.

"Because the guy confessed shortly before he drowned in our pool."

"Jesus, Jax. I don't know what to say."

Her neck is too stiff to turn. She stares ahead: "Andrew is dead."

"What?"

"It's a long story, Chase. I will explain. But not now. I just can't."

"This is all too much to take in, Jax," Fielding says.

"Well, I'm afraid you're going to have to take it in ... because I have spoken to De Pablos."

"You spoke to De Pablos?" To Fielding the idea that she had spoken to De Pablos is impossible. But he can see she is deadly serious. "Go on, Jax. I'm listening."

"You need to contact De Pablos; he expects your call soon. You confirm that Andrew and I had a big fight over something, but everything is ok now. He needs to hear it from you personally. Face Time him so he can see you mean it."

Fielding glances at his watch: "Tonight."

"Also, Griffiths is closing in. He knows about your creative accounting and there is evidence."

"How do you know all this, Jax? How can you?"

"Just trust me, I do. Griffiths is smart."

"Griffiths told you?"

"No, Griffiths is investigating you and he has a bunch of proof."

He looks worried: "Shit."

Jax continues, speaking quietly: "You need to get out of this country and so do I. To Miami, as you and Andrew originally planned ... conspired to ... against me."

Fielding is aghast: "How? How can this possibly work?"

"Leave it to me. I'll call you. But you must reassure this De Pablos character that everything is okay."

"I understand."

"My story to De Pablos was that Andrew was ill in Holland with coronavirus. That's why he was out of contact. You need to support this story. Can you do that?"

"Where was he ill in Holland? A hospital? Hospital admissions can be easily checked. I know that from my contacts at the Norfolk and Norwich."

"I wasn't specific about an actual place. Just a house somewhere in Holland. I'm sure you can concoct something credible. Can you do this? I need to know."

"I told you yes, Jax."

"That way you get your share of the company sale and I get my life back."

"How did Andrew die, Jacqueline?" He's serious; he's used her full name, he never does.

"What do you think? Do you think I would deliberately set out to murder him?"

"No, but all the same ..."

Jax sighs: "I'll call you to finalise arrangements. Lucia will take me to the airport. But you said you'd take me home now."

"That's why I'm here." He glances across at the Dutch rental Peugeot and wonders who it belongs to. Best not to ask too many questions. He is too near serious wealth to care about the details of what really happened to Andrew.

*

The Daimler pulls up on the driveway. Lucia opens the front door of the house looking apprehensive; anxious and fearful of how Jax will treat her after the previous night's revelations.

Before she gets out of the car Jax says: "I'll tell you the whole story in Miami, Chase. Try and keep out of Griffiths' way. He wants blood and he won't stop until he finishes me. And you."

"I've got it. I'll call De Pablos tonight. We're five hours ahead of Miami, so there's time. Look after yourself, Jax."

"I will."

Jax gets out of the Daimler and it immediately pulls away. Much later, Jax would wonder why there was no exchange of pleasantries between Lucia and Chase. Or even an acknowledgement: Maybe they had fallen out and Lucia had simply not bothered to tell her. Another mystery.

Remnants

Brook House, Salhouse, Norfolk

THERE ARE REMNANTS of police crime-scene tape on the driveway and a police car is parked up a hundred feet away. A bored looking 'uniform' at the wheel.

Jax walks up to the open front door to find Lucia standing there looking coy and embarrassed; so, she dives straight in:

"Lucia, I have to try and forget about what you told me last night – at least to try and compartmentalise it – for the time being. D'you understand?"

"Yes."

"I need to forget about Isabelle, Elisabeth and everything. The one thing I've learned through all of this is that I never knew Andrew. He was a stranger who led a whole parallel life I knew nothing about – well, I knew some about – but clearly not all."

"If it's any consolation, Jax, I didn't know him either. And I knew nothing about the car accident and on that I swear my life."

Jax bends her head forward to stretch her neck, in terrible pain. When she looks back up, her eyes are moist with tears: "I have to know I can trust you now more than ever, whatever happens."

"You can."

They stand in silence for a moment then Lucia takes her arm: "You got rid of the Peugeot?"

"Yes, and met Chase in Aylsham ..." She pauses. "... "Chase then dropped me back here as you saw. He's ok and on-side with the plan and will call De Pablos tonight. Come on, I've got stuff to do. Let's just move on. I've got to move on."

Lucia frowns: "By the way, have you seen my Samsung work phone? I seem to have lost it."

*

Later Lucia is sitting in the study. On the desk in front of her are the three crucial pages of computer printout and the soft-leather folder which Jax had discovered in Andrew's attaché case at the Hôtel de L'Europe.

Lucia is looking at the statement from ABN AMRO private banking in Amsterdam and the contract between the Flower Group and De Pablos Corporation in the USA.

Lucia calls out to Jax: "It's just as you said in the car, Jax. To cheat you out of everything, I can't believe what I'm reading."

Jax comes into the study: "I know, and I only found that leather folder by chance." Jax is carrying the contents of Elisabeth's shoulder bag she has retrieved from the wall safe behind the Bugatti painting. This includes the red leather document folder from the Wagner investigators in Berlin:

"Check this out, you might find it interesting after our discussion."

Lucia looks momentarily guarded: "What is it?"

"Everything. All the evidence against Andrew and Chase. And here is Elisabeth's phone ... the messages are damning ...I'm glad I didn't wipe the SIM card that night. I nearly did. And these two photos of me disguised as Eva. Griffiths took them. Look ..."

Lucia sifts through the evidence: "The Spanish dancer?"

"And biker, yes." She pauses. "But Andrew thought I'd never see any of these business papers because I'd be dead. Right, let's put all this together for safety."

"It's still hard to believe he'd do that."

"Really? I'm not so sure now."

Jax puts the soft-leather folder with the AMRO bank statement and De Pablos contract into a strong brown envelope, together with the three pages of computer printout, the two photos and Elisabeth's phone: "I need to keep this lot close, Lu. This is my life from now on." Finally, she adds the Berlin document folder. "And this most important of all, maybe."

"Si. I understand."

"I mustn't forget my Jacqueline Donovitch American passport. I'll run up and get it now."

Missing

Bethel Street Police Station, Main Office, Norwich

MAC AND HELEN are in the main office. Quince comes bounding into the room, clutching a plastic evidence bag and a report from the lab.

"CSI discovered the murdered woman at Brook House has a first name. They found a fine gold bracelet. On the inside of it is an engraving. It says "Elisabeth – aux beaux yeux". No fingerprint ID yet and no blood cross match. Any ideas?"

Quince hands the bag to his team. They examine the bracelet through the cellophane.

Helen translates: "'Elisabeth with the beautiful eyes.' This suggests that she might possibly be French, Belgian, Swiss or from any French-speaking nation."

Quince: "True. Her clothes however appear to be German in origin. The Karl Lagerfeld black blazer she was wearing was purchased from KaDeWe, an upmarket department store in Berlin. The price tag was still clipped inside – eight hundred euros - complete with bar code."

Helen: "Convenient."

"Yes. Or completely accidental," says Quince. "There's nothing else to identify her."

Mac pipes up: "What about the intruder?"

Quince sinks into a chair: "CSI have nothing. Interpol have nothing."

Helen looks into the evidence bag: "Who would give such a gift to a young woman like Elisabeth? It only says she has beautiful eyes; there is no other name."

"Mother? Father? Lover? Could be anyone ... no wedding band, so not a husband," says Quince logically. "Perhaps a very proud French dad." His eyes twinkle. He's an old romantic really.

Helen chuckles: "Exactly the point. Somebody somewhere is going to start missing her. And pretty soon they will report her as such. Either through official channels – like the police – or on social media. I'll keep an eye on the internet. And the news rounds."

Quince gives her an encouraging look: "Good idea, Rossi. Very well thought through."

She flashes Mac a lovely smile: "Thanks, Guv."

Chamois

Brook House, Salhouse, Norfolk

A SOLITARY KNOCK ON THE DOOR. Jax looks through the peep-hole and opens the front door to find Quince, clutching a freshly packaged chamois leather. She smiles warmly at him, completely surprised.

"I thought this might come in handy for leathering the TR off. I tend to use the car wash now for my old motor."

"Quince. That's very thoughtful and kind."

"How are you? Dumb question but an obvious one."

She pulls the collar of her polo neck down so he can see her bruises: "Look. And I'm stiff all over from the fall."

"Nasty."

Jax painfully rotates her head: "It is but I'll live. Won't you come in?"

"Just for a minute."

"Follow me."

*

They walk into the study and make themselves comfortable; he in a leather armchair and she on the stool by the desk. Elgar's cello concerto plays softly in the background.

"Ah, Jacqueline du Pré. Magnificent."

"I adore her playing, her skill. I tried to learn cello once, I was useless. Piano is my thing." She gives him a warm smile and, for a moment, share the music.

Quince nods, then steeples his hands, tone formal: "Mrs Flower. Have you any idea who the intruder was or why he was in your house?"

"All I can think is that he came to steal a car – he saw the woman – thought she was the householder and killed her in panic ... I disturbed him ... caught him in the act."

Quince purses his lips doubtfully: "He was armed with a Glock 17M, that's pretty impressive hardware for a car thief."

She raises her eyebrows: "I don't really know what that is - a gun, I guess."

Quince sighs: "Yes. A 9mm semi-automatic pistol. Austrian, military, unusual."

"What does that mean? I don't follow."

"It means, Mrs Flower, your intruder was a professional. It is the sort used by the military and FBI ... he must have very good contacts to source that sort of gun."

Jax gulps audibly: "That makes it even more scary."

Quince leans forward: "I know it does. The whole episode is scary, as you say ... You see the magazine capacity is 17 rounds, and yet it was only loaded with six."

"All he thought he'd need?" Jax asks with an audible shiver.

"Exactly."

She suddenly stands: "Would you like a drink, Quince? I often have a JD at this hour."

"I would love to – but I have the wheels – and I'm a policeman after all. It wouldn't be setting a good example." His tone is jovial, yet he is serious.

Jax laughs: "Did you really have other business in Amsterdam when you collected the Audi?"

He matches her gaze: "No."

"Then why?"

Quince takes a breath: "Because I sense a vulnerability ... something in your eyes. And I feel you have been through ... something. Not recently, perhaps in the past. Despite all you have, it hasn't been plain sailing for you."

"That's very intuitive." Jax says, heartfelt.

Quince starts to stand to face her: "I wanted to help you."

"And you did." Now their faces are a foot apart. She gazes at him. "And I am grateful."

"Good." There is a sudden frisson between them, but Quince knows the boundaries.

"Stay and have a drink, just one. I promise not to put you over the limit."

"I'd love to, but I mustn't for a galaxy of reasons." The last few words come out in a tuneful Celtic rhythm, almost melodic.

"Pity."

"'Tis the way of the world, and I'm afraid I must go." He

pauses: "I have your mobile number. I'll keep you posted."

Quince holds out his hand, which she takes, then kisses him on the cheek: "Please do ... and thank you ... Come on, I'll walk you out."

They walk through the house in silence to the front door, then say a brief farewell. Quince walks down the driveway towards his battered old Renault. Jax remains standing there and notices she is still holding the chamois.

Travel Case

Brook House. Jax's Dressing Room, Salhouse, Norfolk

JAX QUIETLY PACKS A red travel case: a blue and red striped blazer and lightweight chinos. She tucks a pair of aviator-style glasses niftily into the top pocket of the blazer. Then on top she places a skirt, blouses, and some underwear. She takes a capacious sponge bag marked KYROLAN MAKE-UP and carefully packs the same items of make-up and accessories for disguise which she'd used before in Amsterdam. She buries them all deep inside the bag and covers them with pairs of knickers, nylons and a box of opened Tampax.

She is ticking off the items on a mental 'to do' list. Inside the padded lid of the travel case is an inlaid vanity mirror. Jax slices the fabric above the mirror open with a razor blade. She slips Andrew's passport into the gap behind and pushes down. It's a tight fit but concealed. She wipes the mirror clean of smudges and zips the case.

A few minutes later, in the hallway of Brook House, Jax puts the strong brown envelope into a sturdy canvas carrier and picks up the bottle of Château Latour 1982, still unopened from the night of their wedding anniversary. Lucia watches her with intrigue.

"I can't bear to part with this, it has significance."

"You might have to." Lucia wheels the red travel case to the doorway and turns, "Do you have everything?"

Jax: "Oh no. I haven't! Thank you. I almost forgot. Have a look in the cupboard under the kitchen sink. You'll find a carrier bag ... go and get it for me, will you?"

Lucia appears a few moments later: "Feels heavy, what's in it?"

"Fifty-seven thousand euros – less ten for a cab fare in Amsterdam – and twenty thousand bucks."

Lucia looks amazed: "A fortune!"

Jax takes the carrier: "Why would Andrew need that much cash? Most people use credit cards these days, don't they?"

Lucia huffs: "Only the black market deals in cash, Jax."

Jax sighs: "Hmm. True. There was a guy outside the Tulip on Gravenstraat – and then he appeared again on, where was it, Damrak, speaking on a mobile phone. I noticed him out the corner of my eye. Thought nothing of it at the time."

"And?" says Lucia, looking at her watch.

"I don't know, maybe there's a connection? Not sure. Black market? We certainly know Andrew's proclivities, don't we, Lu?

… I'll put this money in with the rest of the stuff."

Lucia ignores the jibe: "Twenty thousand dollars will help settle a few hotel bills in Miami, Jax."

"Yeah, it will buy me a few Jack Daniels too … Come on, we need to get to the airport."

They drive away in Lucia's VW and a moment later the illuminated driveway fades to black.

Photograph

Bethel Street Police Station Car Park, Norwich

QUINCE IS ABOUT TO GET into his Renault Clio. Mac comes running out to catch him before he leaves. He is clutching a printed email.

Mac is breathless from running: "Guv! Guv! Guv!"

"What is it, Mac? I'm on another mission - it's black with a white head this time – served in a pint glass. It has my name on it."

"You won't believe this, Guv. An email from the German Police, Berlin. A missing person."

Quince shuts the door to his car, turns round, immediately interested: "My Guinness can wait."

"Her name is Elisabeth Deluc. And there is a very grainy passport photo of her. It's her, I'm sure of it. The dead woman in the kitchen – Elisabeth with the beautiful eyes."

Quince exhales doubtfully: "But Deluc doesn't sound very German. French maybe? Belgian?"

"But her clothes were purchased in Berlin, remember?

KaDeWe, the expensive department store." He pauses for a second. "Can't be a coincidence, can it?"

"No, you're right. Email them back. See if you can get a decent photo ID of this Elisabeth Deluc. Good job, Mac."

Mac remembers Rossi's lovely smile the other day: "Thanks, Guv."

Airport

Norwich International Airport, Amsterdam Way, Norwich

THE DEPARTURES AREA, just before Passport Control, is busy with passengers. Jax has her red travel case, the sturdy canvas carrier and her handbag. She clutches her boarding pass and passport anxiously. Lucia and she are talking. Two Customs officers approach them.

The first officer is polite, but formal: "Mrs Flower? Jacqueline Flower?"

Jax looks at Lucia as if to say what's happening: "Yes."

He flicks his ID: "Would you mind, please?"

Jax is mystified: "Is there a problem?"

A door from the HM Revenue & Customs airport office opens and Hywel Griffiths appears, business like: "Problem is perhaps my favourite word."

He acknowledges Lucia; notices the bottle neck protruding from the canvas carrier they packed at the house: "We meet again, Mrs. Flower. How nice."

Jax is shocked, can't hide it. But Griffiths is in his element. He glances at the carrier: "What's this?" Griffiths leans forward; removes the bottle from the carrier. The moment is loaded: all the evidence Griffiths needs to detain Jax is in the brown envelope in that carrier. Plus, the unaccounted-for cash. Jax and Lucia freeze as Griffiths admires the label: "Hm, Château Latour 1982. Nice." He eyes Jax and Lucia and sighs: "When was the last time you travelled by air, Mrs Flower?"

"I can't remember." She looks desperately at Lucia for some sort of guidance.

Griffiths continues: "The regulations have changed concerning fluids. There's ample warning all over the airport ... and on-line, of course."

Lucia jumps in: "But this carrier is mine and so is the wine, for my husband. So, if you wouldn't mind giving it to me, please. I'm not travelling." Lucia takes the bottle from Griffiths and places it back into the canvas carrier, giving the impression it all belongs to her. Her face betrays nothing. "Thank you."

Griffiths turns to Jax: "Say goodbye to your friend, Mrs Flower. We need to speak." He walks back to the office door, leaving Jax and Lucia speechless. The two Customs officers stand by.

Jax: "Thanks for the lift, Lu. I'll text you." They embrace guardedly as the men step forward.

Lucia hurries off with the carrier, not daring to looking back.

*

The two officers accompany Jax and her red travel case into a stark office, by the inspection area. A female Customs officer and Griffiths are standing there:

"Is this all your baggage then, Mrs Flower?" The merest hint of South Glamorgan and a glint in his eye.

Jax nods as Griffiths lifts her travel case onto an inspection counter. He opens the case and starts to search. Inside he finds her skirt, blouses, underwear and the Kyrolan sponge bag which he unzips. He sees make-up accessories, knickers, and the box of opened Tampax. He dismisses these personal items, slightly embarrassed, zips it up and puts it to one side on the counter. Jax watches intently.

He delves deeper into the case and discovers the blazer and lightweight chinos. He pokes his hand into the blazer's top pocket and pulls out the aviator-style glasses with a silver frame. He lifts a necktie up and looks at her suspiciously: "What are you doing with men's clothing, Mrs Flower?" His tone is now provocative.

She retorts: "It's my husband's travel case too, you know."

He probes her further: "You hoping to see him soon then, are you?"

"Oh, I will see him."

He turns to the female Customs officer: "Search her, if you please. You're entitled to a second chaperone if you want one, Mrs Flower."

The officer steps forward, presenting a warrant, as part of

correct procedure.

Jax is indignant: "I don't want one. Search me."

The female Customs officer leads her away towards an examination room. Griffiths and the two male Customs officers watch them disappear. Griffiths sifts through Jax's red travel case one last time, hoping to find something, anything incriminating. But he can't. Lucia has it all. A few moments later the female Customs emerges, shaking her head at Griffiths: nothing.

"Right, I'll need to speak to Quince. Tomorrow. He'll know something, I'm sure." His words have more than an edge: he knows that somehow, he's been outwitted.

The Customs officers watch Griffiths disappear from the inspection area with an air of finality.

*

At airport departures, Lucia looks up at the display board depicting international departures and arrivals:

KLM: NORWICH TO AMSTERDAM –
DEPARTED.

Lucia watches a plane take off and wonders if Jax is on it. Or was Griffiths able to detain her longer than he needed to? As she passes a waste bin, she drops the unopened bottle of Château Latour into it with a heartfelt sigh. It drops to the bottom with a decisive clunk:

"Goodbye Mr Flower."

Twenty-Four Hours Later

Bethel Street Police Station, Norwich

QUINCE, MAC AND HELEN are in the main office. WPC Judith Clarke comes in enthusiastically, clutching a phone: "Guv! Cas Van Der Maas, says it's important."

Quince jumps up expectantly to take the call. His team's eyes are all fixed on him. He presses the speaker button: "Cas! Some news from my favourite city?"

"Hey! Quince. Yes! Andrew Flower turned up again here this morning."

Quince is surprised: "Really?"

Cas laughs: "Echt! Echt! Really, truly, genuinely. Look at your computer screen now."

Quince flicks his fingers to get Helen to fire up his computer and says: "Face Time!", excitedly.

After a few moments, the screen of his Mac divides into two halves. On the left-hand side, Cas is on the phone. On the right is CCTV footage of a man. He is at the ticket office of an airport railway station, buying a ticket: he's about forty, with sandy-brown hair and a neatly-styled goatee beard. He wears aviator-style glasses; he's dressed in a blue and red striped blazer and chinos.

Cas continues: "Andrew Flower bought a first-class rail ticket at Schiphol airport, using a Visa credit card. The transaction was verified by a four-digit pin number. I have an enlarged picture of him on my desk." He pauses to let it sink in: "It's a positive ID as far as I'm concerned, Quince. Destination Frankfurt."

Mac, Helen and Clarke all remain silent, watching the screen and listening.

Quince: "You had his name flagged on your system, did you? I didn't realise."

Cas responds: "Yes. But you didn't want him stopped, did you? As far as we're concerned, he was simply another missing person ... misper, yes ..."

Quince: "No. I didn't want him stopped."

Cas is upbeat: "So then, he's not missing anymore. Now Quince, watch this CCTV from the arrivals area at Schiphol yesterday evening." Quince and his team watch Jax pulling her red travel case behind her. "Can you see this?"

"Yes."

"Mrs Jacqueline Flower arrived from Norwich yesterday. The KLM City Hopper to Schiphol. Maybe Mr & Mrs Flower are hoping to meet up?"

The assembled group hang on every word, captivated by the images.

Quince sounds surprised: "You had her name flagged too?"

Cas laughs again: "No! The name 'Flower' came up as an alert because of her husband. That's all."

Quince looks at the others again: "I see."

"Anyway, your mystery is now solved ... I have to go, Quince. Inspector Joop van Durren is looking at me through the glass. Gemeentepolitie is chaotic today." The line goes dead.

Quince, Mac, Helen and Judith are dumbfounded by the sudden silence. The atmosphere is broken by the sound of knocking on the door and Hywel Griffiths entering simultaneously.

He is suddenly standing there uninvited: "DI Quince. You look pale. I'll need a full update if you don't mind. Have there been any developments I need to know about?"

Quince looks at Mac and Helen: "Ah, Mr Griffiths, delightful to see you. How timely. Superintendent Brian Cragg – our boss – is after you."

Griffiths looks alarmed: "Really?"

"Hamish Mulvey, HMRC Compliance Enforcement Division telephoned him earlier. Apparently, there's to be an enquiry into your moonlighting as a private detective." Quince can't resist a very slight smile. And neither can the others.

But Griffiths is utterly crestfallen: "An enquiry, is it?"

"Yes, Mr Griffiths. HMRC don't approve of their inspectors having a second job, on their time, and using HM Government ID to gain access to exclusive areas."

The timing couldn't have been better as Cragg enters the room to join them. He looks at Quince and the others, then Griffiths: "And there's been an accusation of assault, Mr

Griffiths. Unsubstantiated, of course. But by a Spanish national. A lady by the name of Eva Flores. Ring any bells?"

Griffiths stumbles: "No." But there is a flicker of recognition in his eyes: he has heard the name before, and he has certainly seen her.

Helen pipes up: "Sir, Eva Flores is a famous Spanish dancer. Everybody knows who she is."

"Well, I don't," says Griffiths. "Never heard of her."

Cragg continues: "Anyway, she phoned HMRC at 100 Parliament Street London and made a formal complaint to their HR department." Cragg pauses a moment. "You need to contact this Mulvey character, pronto. You can use my office. This way, please."

Griffiths has been shot down in flames, but turns to Quince: "Is this your doing, Quince?"

But before Quince can answer Cragg raises his voice with authority: "Mr Griffiths ... this way if you please. I haven't got all day ... and I doubt Officer Mulvey has either."

Fever

Intercity Train:
Amsterdam to Frankfurt, Germany

JAX STARES INTO THE MIRROR of a toilet cubicle in an intercity train. First, she removes the aviator-style glasses and wig. Then she very carefully peels off the goatee beard, wary of the sticky spirit gum. Next is the crêpe hair for the eyebrows and lastly the latex nose. She places all the items back into the Kyrolan sponge bag.

The transformation takes her twenty minutes. She has to swop clothes in the very cramped space, from the blazer and chinos into her own. And then repack. This will be the last time; the final alibi is cemented.

Jax feels woozy: Is it the motion of the train, the anticipation of escape to Miami or a malaise gripping her? She feels dizzy and weak. Her throat feels sore and dry, and her head is pounding. Her pulse is racing, and the back of her neck is damp with perspiration. She thinks: Oh great. I'm getting sick with a virus, but I must catch that flight.

She lets herself out of the cubicle, struggles back into the carriage and sits down, still carefully guarding her red travel case.

TRAIN ANNOUNCER:
'Our final station is Frankfurt. One hour.'

She settles back and immediately falls into a deep, troubled sleep; a confused theatre of random characters haunt her: Elisabeth, Andrew, Nigel and Lucia, her best friend. Could she ever forgive her for what she did all those years ago? Maybe her mama would give her the answer from beyond.

*

On arrival at Frankfurt Hbf, she takes a deep breath and gets off the train, grateful for fresh air. She decides against the S-Bahn and finds a taxi to take her to the airport. She knows she has to rally.

In the back of the taxi, she feels giddy, and her body is burning up. She states her destination and immediately falls asleep again.

After a few moments the driver asks if she is alright: "Geht es Ihnen gut?"

"I'm American. How far is the airport?" Her voice sounds weak and reedy.

"Nine kilometres – twenty minutes or more." He glances at her in the rear-view mirror. "It depends on the traffic as always."

"I need aspirin. Can we stop at a pharmacy?"

The driver opens his glove box and produces a sealed sachet marked 'Bayer Aspirin.' He passes it back through the plastic payment slot: "Take two of these ... you have water?"

Jax holds up a bottle of Apollinaris German mineral water: "Yes, thank you. I'll pay you for them."

He laughs: "Nein! Bitte! Sit back. Relax."

She does just that.

Flight

Lufthansa Frankfurt to Miami LH 462

JAX SITS BACK IN THE LUXURY of business class on the Boeing 747-830 and tries to savour the moment. When she was young, she fantasised about flying in an airplane. But now she doesn't feel well. As a child she'd lie in her single bed at home, staring up at the ceiling. She'd watch patterns and shadows dancing above her and wonder what lay ahead for her. Would she be happy, or would she be sad?

At Frankfurt airport she'd dosed up on Vitamin C, echinacea and more aspirin. She closes her eyes. On the threshold of sleep, she clutches her iPhone, even though she switched it off. She sits there alone suddenly realising she may have lost everything. It all depends on her convincing De Pablos.

She opens her eyes; a man is walking down the aisle wearing a blazer and chinos. For a split second she's convinced it's Andrew and starts to panic. She blinks and he's gone. Obviously, a mirage; an optical illusion brought on by the fever: the palms of her hands are moist with sweat.

A steward approaches: "May I get you a drink, Ma'am? Or anything?"

"Maybe in a while."

"Are you alright?"

She summons a smile: "I'm not a good traveller."

The steward nods in understanding and Jax settles back again. Her eyes take her to the cabin divider. It suddenly opens, and a solitary figure walks towards her: the shoes are Gucci. Jax thinks she is delirious. Then she sees a pair of black georgette pario trousers by Versace and a medusa cardigan over a white silk blouse. The features are obscured by a face mask, but her bearing is familiar ...

A brown envelope is placed onto Jax's lap, immediately recognisable. Jax looks down at it and then up at the figure, absolutely stunned. It can only be one person and Jax can hardly get her name out. This cannot be real: she's hallucinating again. But she tries:

"Lu?"

Lucia pulls the mask down: "I got a return ticket on standby. Last one. Luck was on my side, for once."

"I can't believe it ... after everything."

Jax stands up awkwardly: "I won't get too near you, I'm unwell." She grabs hold of the precious envelope and holds it close to her chest like a baby. Tears fill her eyes.

"So am I, that's why I'm wearing this mask."

Jax sits down in the window seat: "I just can't believe you're here, with this."

"But I am here, Jax."

"My God ... No problem with Griffiths at the airport then?"

Lucia shakes her head and sits beside her: "No. It was you he wanted to catch, Jax. And he didn't. He was envious of you, resentful."

"Do you know what I still don't understand?" Jax pauses to compose her thoughts. "If Griffiths is a genuine tax inspector - which I guess he must be - what was he doing at Schiphol with Elisabeth Deluc? A private investigator and, what, a civil servant."

"That was the first question you posed that day in the car, when you came back from Holland."

Jax: "Yeah, I remember, Lu. It had me foxed then and it still does. I guess we'll never know what their connection is."

Lucia gives her a sideways glance: "No, I guess we never will."

VOICE OVER/CABIN CREW: 'Please ensure smartphones and electronic devices are switched to airplane mode during this flight. Thank you.'

Jax turns her iPhone on; and it bleeps with a message that was received three hours previously UK time: "Jacqueline. It's Quince. We've had a positive ID of the dead woman. Elisabeth Deluc, a Belgian national from Bruges. Ironically, she was reported missing by a German in Berlin. A Kurt Wagner ... very worried about her ..."

Jax turns to Lucia: She can't believe Quince has discovered so much already.

Images

Quince's office, Bethel Street Police Station, Norwich

QUINCE SITS AT HIS DESK. He's holding the plastic evidence bag containing Elisabeth's bracelet. On his desk is a printed email from Wilhelm Wehrmann and Kurt Wagner, Private Investigators, with a photograph of Elisabeth. But he is transfixed by the images he sees on his computer screen.

Quince continues with his message to Jax: "... yes, Kurt Wagner is very worried about her. We'll find out more in time. Oh, I've got another bit of news as well. But don't worry, it can wait ..."

Quince looks at CCTV footage Mac and Rossi have compiled. Images – on screen - from the Dorchester Hotel's main reception: Jax and Lucia talking to the cashier and settling their bill with VISA. Then Andrew Flower buying a ticket at Schiphol airport railway station. He's seen some of it before, but this time it's more interesting.

" ... Have a good trip to Miami. Oh, and don't forget to come home, Mrs Flower. Your TR4A will need washing soon. Lucky you have a nice new chamois to leather it!" Quince grins and hangs up.

Holiday

Lufthansa Frankfurt to Miami LH 462

THE STEWARD REAPPEARS and sees Lucia sitting beside Jax. He addresses her courteously:

"Ready for that drink now, Ma'am?"

Jax acknowledges the steward with a nod, but it still feels painful: "Jack Daniels on the rocks, please."

Lucia smiles: "Campari, ice and grapefruit juice, please."

The steward smiles: "Coming up."

Lucia turns to her friend: "Can you forgive me, Jax? If not, I'll stand and go back to my seat in the other cabin."

"Forgiveness will help me repair our friendship, Lu. It's the only way I can reconcile."

Lucia grips hold of Jax's forearm: "I don't want to lose you."

"I know, Lu, I know ... I need a little time, I guess."

A few moments later the steward arrives with their drinks: crystal glasses and delicious looking appetisers. Finally, they toast and savour the moment: they are here, after all.

"What do you think will happen, Jax? When we get to

Florida?"

Jax sighs deeply: "At least I'll try and get Brook House back, Lu. Or try and persuade De Pablos not to sell it. It's down to them, I guess." She pauses and considers. "After everything, I must try. I owe it to myself."

"Christopher?" Lucia asks.

"I've arranged to meet him at the Biltmore Hotel, Coral Gables, Miami. Three days' time. He's organised a get-together with De Pablos, father and son. I've got work to do and I hope I feel better than I do now. Maybe I'll try and sweat it out in the hotel sauna."

"Well, you can work, Jax. I need a holiday. I'm exhausted."

Jax is incredulous: "Ha! You need a holiday ... that's rich!"

"I've had quite a week of it, you know ..." Lucia sees the ice is starting to melt ... "all in all."

"Yeah ... so have I," says Jax, "all in all."

Lucia finishes her drink: "I must freshen up." She stands and walks down the aisle towards the rest room, carrying her Lufthansa in-flight 'Amenity Kit.' Jax sits back, closes her eyes, tries to relax, then hears the steward trying to gain her attention:

"Sorry to disturb you, ma'am, your friend dropped her ticket." He holds it out for her to take.

"Yeah, she was lucky," says Jax. "She got a return ticket on standby. Last one, apparently. Thanks a lot."

The steward looks at the ticket, mystified: "That would be highly unusual. This was probably purchased months ago. Besides, our flight isn't full today, for a change," he chuckles, "less work for me and the girls." He hands Jax Lucia's ticket and scurries off back to the galley. She stares at it in disbelief, the same ticket as Andrew's and Elisabeth's: FRANKFURT TO MIAMI, BUSINESS CLASS. LH 462. Name of Passenger: Lucia Paluzzi.

She swallows as the acid taste of betrayal rises in her throat. She reaches down into the canvas carrier. Her hands are shaking. She sees the bundles of cash and two mobile phones; she knows one is Elisabeth's. The other is Lucia's spare Samsung for work. The one she said she'd lost. Slowly she opens the leather case and enters Lucia's pin code ...

Quickly she checks the aisle, heart pounding, flicks to WhatsApp; last message on Chats from Christopher Fielding:

> *My masonic friend Dr Rix, District Coroner, has concocted and issued Andrew's Death Certificate: lost at sea. Six originals. One has been sent to the Registrar. Another has been couriered to ABN AMRO bank in Amsterdam, together with a signed affidavit from me. They will transfer £10M to Banque Privée in the Caymans. It's all dropped right into our laps, Lu. We'll have to work out what to do about Jax. See you in Miami. Miss you. Christopher xx*

She sinks into her seat as Lucia walks back down the aisle and sees the ashen pallor of Jax's face.

THE END

Thank You

Especially to my wife Pam for her love and patience; and to Marianne, always my first and trusted reader.

To J.P. for such a great edit and for providing so many creative suggestions.

Len Greenwood for the original artwork and continued enthusiasm for the Valentine Series and all my other writing projects.

To all my readers who have written such great reviews for all my work to date.

Margaret Mitchell ITV Producer who read through a draft screenplay of 'Jax' and gave me guidance about structure and story arc.

Alex Matthews for the police and crime scene procedure.

Steffi Berghmans of Kryolan Professional Make-up specialists, for help on Jax's make-over.

Steve New for advising on the technical aspects of an abattoir.

Cheryl Oakley, Stena Ferry Line, Harwich.

Sam Snape, BAFTA, for helping me develop the story originally.

II

A Note from the Author

'Jacqueline with flowers' was painted by Picasso in 1954 and introduced his companion Jacqueline Roque.

I have borrowed her surname for my character Clémence Roque in my forthcoming book: *The Revenge Of Catherine Delane*. I thought the coincidence too delicious not to be mentioned! '*Revenge*' features many of the characters who appear in '*Betrayal*' and will be published soon.

Robert Wallace

March 2023.

Printed in Great Britain
by Amazon

50488441R00136